THE DAY the World WENT LOKI

Kelpies is an imprint of Floris Books

First published in 2013 by Floris Books
© 2013 Robert J. Harris
Second printing 2014

Robert J. Harris has asserted his right under the
Copyright, Designs and Patent Act 1988 to be identified
as the Author of this work

The publisher acknowledges subsidy from
Creative Scotland towards the publication
of this volume

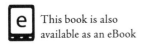 This book is also
available as an eBook

British Library CIP data available
ISBN 978-178250-030-8
Printed in Great Britain
by DS Smith Print Solutions, Glasgow

Robert J. Harris

 Kelpies

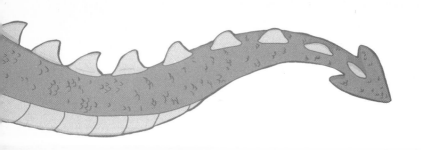

To my sons, Matthew, Rob and Jamie.
They never got into this much trouble.

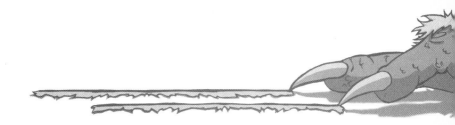

1. BAD LUCK AND

WORSE LUCK

Neither of the boys strolling home from Madras High School in St Andrews had any idea that this was just about the last normal day of their lives. Greg McBride had something else on his mind.

"A maths test *tomorrow!*" he exploded. "How's that for bad luck?" He swung an angry fist through the empty air. "But then bad luck is all I ever get."

His younger brother Lewis made an absent-minded humming noise as he braced himself for more complaints. It was a long walk down Lamond Drive, but it seemed twice as long when Greg was on one of his rants.

"Some folk get hit singles, star in films, run big companies, but not me. Oh no, I never get that kind of luck."

"It's not luck," Lewis murmured.

"Huh?" Greg grunted. He hadn't expected Lewis to say anything. He usually didn't until his older brother had quite finished. "What are you mumbling about?"

"Maybe it's not just luck," Lewis said. He wished heartily that he hadn't opened his mouth, but now he had no choice but to tough it out. "Maybe they're successful because they work hard."

Greg shook his head. "If all it took was hard work, then everybody who worked hard would be rich. But they're not, are they?"

"I suppose not."

"You suppose not," Greg echoed mockingly. "That's your trouble, Lewis. You don't think things through. I mean, what chance have I got living here? St Andrews isn't exactly the centre of the universe, is it? It's not even the centre of Fife."

A large shadow passed over them as their enormous friend Arthur "the Chiz" Chisholm came loping by. "Guys," he rumbled by way of greeting.

The Chiz had pulled on his favourite red beanie with one hand so that it lay squint across the crown of his head like a UFO that had crash landed on a mountain peak.

"Hi, Chiz," the brothers responded as their friend's long strides carried him swiftly past them.

"Hey, Chiz, do you want to kick a ball around?" Greg called after him.

Kicking a ball around with the Chiz mostly involved searching for the ball after he'd booted it thirty metres through the air in the wrong direction. Still, it was better than studying for a test.

Chiz glanced back over his shoulder. "Home... work... test tomorrow," he answered. Every word sounded like an echo in a coal mine.

He loped off and left Greg grimacing. "Even Chiz'll probably pass," he said. "You'd think they'd hang a big sign up to remind you a test is coming. I mean, what is the point of mentioning it weeks ago, in the middle of class when nobody's paying any attention, then never talking about it again until the day before? How is anybody supposed to remember something like that?"

There was a merciful thirty seconds of silence as they held their noses while passing Canny Dan's Snack Van. As soon as they were clear of the stench of grease, pickled onion and charred black pudding, Greg resumed.

"I'll bet Mrs Witherspoon kept this test a secret just to trip me up. She's always had it in for me."

"You mean because you never do any work."

"No, it's something more personal than that. She'd hang me up and use me for target practice if she thought she'd get away with it."

"You could still get a good four or five hours of studying in tonight," Lewis pointed out. "That might be enough."

"Is that right?" Greg answered with undisguised sarcasm. "You think it's that easy to study, like you can just sit down and do it? Have you learned nothing? You have to plan it in advance, draw up a timetable, or you might as well not bother."

"So you're not going to bother?"

"I didn't say that, I was just making a point. For your benefit, I might add."

At the corner of Largo Road he pulled up short as Lindsay Jensen popped up in front of him, as though out of thin air.

"Hi, Greg!" she beamed, like she hadn't seen him in years.

Her corn-coloured hair was tied in a ponytail with a pink ribbon. Behind her gold-rimmed glasses her eyes shone like sapphires, at least that's how they looked to Lewis.

"Oh hi, Lindsay," Greg responded distractedly. He was peering around from side to side, trying to figure out where she could have sprung from. She had an unsettling knack for ambushes.

Lewis cleared his throat. "Hello, Lindsay. That's a really pretty necklace you're wearing." He sighed when he realised that she hadn't even heard him. She was too busy watching Greg scratch his head.

"I hear your dad's gone away on a trip," Lindsay said.

"He's in Wales," said Greg, not meeting her gaze.

"Building a golf course," Lewis added, unnoticed.

Lindsay was in Lewis' class at school, but she only had eyes for his brother. Greg was a year older, taller, thought himself much better looking, and was definitely a lot louder.

"Greg, do you fancy going to that new 3D film tonight?" Lindsay asked breathlessly. "You know, the one about the dancing robots and the polar bear. It looks magic."

"I've got a big test tomorrow," Greg muttered, trying to manoeuvre around her. Lindsay moved expertly to block him.

"I could help you study, Greg," she offered sweetly.

"Lewis is helping me," Greg told her flatly. He grabbed Lewis by the arm and accelerated past her, dragging his brother behind him. Once they were across the street he asked out of the side of his mouth, "Is she gone?"

"Yes, she's gone," Lewis admitted glumly. "She's headed off into town with some of her pals."

"She must be a Japanese ninja or something," mused Greg. "That's the only way she could sneak up on us like that."

"Actually, I think Jensen is a Norwegian name."

"Norwegians don't sneak, Lewis, they ski. Everybody

knows that. And that reminds me, where did you sneak off to at break time?"

"I ran down to the library to get a couple of books Mr Calvert said he'd look out for me."

"More books? What are you doing? Building a castle out of them?"

"They're about time. It's for my school project."

"Time?" snorted Greg. "That's just what I need – more time."

He snatched a book that was sticking out of the top of Lewis' bag and squinted at the faded letters on the cover. "*The Folklore Of Time* by Lucas Oberon Key," he read out. "Maybe there are some tips in this."

"Give that back," said Lewis. He made a grab for the book but Greg whipped it away. "Mr Calvert says it's very rare."

"Mr Calvert says, Mr Calvert says," Greg echoed mockingly. "If I had a pound for every time I've heard you say that, I could buy the school and close it down."

Lewis shoved his fists into his pockets and trudged on with his head down.

"Hmm... it says here the ancient Egyptians had ten days of the week," said Greg, "and that in parts of Africa they have three, four or five days."

Lewis kept up a tight-lipped, silent protest as Greg flicked haphazardly through the old book.

As soon as they turned the corner into Bannock Street the Larkins' dog started barking its head off behind their two-metre high garden fence. The dog had got loose more times than anybody could count, even though the Larkins had done everything to keep it from escaping, short of putting up a guard tower and searchlights.

"Did you know that in 1752 they dropped eleven days from the calendar in England," Greg laughed, "and people rioted in the streets because they wanted their days back?"

"I know," Lewis burst out. "They were changing over from the Julian to the Gregorian calendar. That's part of my project, remember?"

"I know how they felt," said Greg. "I'd give a lot for just one extra day." He turned the page and a huge grin spread across his face. "Say, here's something *really* interesting."

Whatever he was about to say, the words died on his lips and both boys froze in terror when they saw what was parked in the driveway of their house.

Aunt Vivien's car.

Numbly Greg closed the book and handed it back. "Lewis," he said, "I want you to take this book and beat me to death with it."

2. BANQUET OF THE DOOMED

Lewis pushed the book back into his bag. "If you think I'm going in there by myself," he said, "you're off your head."

The boys could not have been more shocked if they'd come home to find Godzilla sitting on the roof, picking his teeth with the TV aerial.

There was no mistaking that bright green Morris Minor, a make of car most scientists were agreed had been extinct since the late Triassic. The purple dice hanging over the dashboard and the toy nodding dog scowling from the rear window were proof that it could only belong to Aunt Vivien.

They stood a while longer in silent terror, then eventually Greg said, "You go in first."

"Why me?" Lewis' voice was almost a shriek.

"You're smaller. It'll be easier for you to slip past her. I'll be right behind you."

With a fatalistic shake of the head Lewis squared his shoulders and walked up the front path. Greg followed a couple of paces behind. By the time they reached the door, Lewis had twisted the straps of his bag so tightly around his fingers that they had turned white.

"Go on," Greg urged. "Look, if we can make it upstairs, we can take turns hiding in the bathroom."

Lewis reached out and took a tentative grip on the doorknob. He turned it slowly, then pushed the door open and made a mad dash for the stairs.

Aunt Vivien was waiting in the hallway and he ran headlong into an embrace that could have suffocated a rhino.

"Boys!" warbled Aunt Vivien in a voice that sent a cold shiver down their spines. "I've been waiting for you to get home!"

With a mammoth effort Lewis struggled free and staggered back, colliding with Greg who had come to a stunned halt just inside the doorway.

There she was, Aunt Vivien, large as life and about as welcome as a plague of midgies, teetering on a pair of high-heeled shoes. Her bosom heaved with emotion beneath a tent-like dress so garishly floral it almost made their eyes scream with pain. Her red-dyed hair was piled high upon her head like something constructed by the pharaohs.

"Come and have a hug, Greg!" she commanded with a falsetto warmth that didn't mask the cold steel beneath. It was hard to tell if she was smiling under all that make-up.

Her open arms were about as inviting as the gaping jaws of a crocodile. Even in her stiletto heels she was still shorter than Greg, but she seemed to fill the space around her like a balloon inflating out of control. She took a purposeful step towards him.

Greg stood paralysed for a moment, trying to control his panic. Then all at once he started to sneeze.

The sneeze arrested Aunt Vivien in mid-step. Her painted mouth formed a horrified O and she retreated a pace, groping for a handkerchief to cover her nose and mouth.

Much as he resented his brother's escape, Lewis couldn't help but admire his quick thinking. Aunt Vivien hated any sort of illness and from the look on her face you'd have thought Greg was carrying the Black Death into the house.

As they trooped into the living room, Aunt Vivien pointed a finger at Greg. "Greg, I can fix you a remedy that will knock those germs right out of you."

Greg blanched at the threat. He didn't doubt for a moment that she could concoct a brew that would flush the marrow out of his bones.

"I'll be all right," he assured her. He sneezed again to be on the safe side. "Just let me get a sandwich."

He headed for the kitchen, making sure to keep the sofa between himself and Aunt Vivien as extra insurance against her unwanted attentions.

"I don't think you'll want to spoil your appetite," she warned. She raised her pencilled eyebrows meaningfully as she spoke. "I have a treat in store for you."

Lewis felt his stomach lurch as he followed Greg into the kitchen.

Even from behind Mum had the dejected appearance of a prisoner of war being subjected to forced labour. Her light brown hair was tied back in a tight, efficient bun and she was wearing the "practical" blue and white striped apron she only wore when she was doing something truly tragic like cleaning out the rubbish bins. She turned from the sink to greet Greg and Lewis as they walked in.

"Hello, boys. Did you have a good day at school?"

She summoned a fragile smile in an unconvincing pretence of normality. But the kitchen was not normal. It had been invaded by something that would blight their lives and their digestion for weeks to come, and there was no way to escape its malignant influence.

Only one thing about Aunt Vivien's visits inspired more outright fear than the lady herself – her cookbook. There it squatted on the kitchen counter like an enormous, leering toad, its ancient cover a hundred mottled shades of brown.

Once, perhaps, it had been an ordinary cookbook, such as you might find in any happy kitchen, but that must have been centuries ago, back when the whole world was a more innocent place. Since then it had been stained and befouled with every manner of spice, sauce and condiment. Fragments of ill-smelling herbs were trapped between the ragged pages, all of which were scrawled with helpful hints in Aunt Vivien's spidery hand. Some of the recipes had been borrowed from the savage tribes of Borneo and the Amazon jungles, while others were best suited to the minutes of a war crimes tribunal.

Lewis wrenched his eyes away from the book and said, "School was okay, Mum. You know."

Mum was washing something sticky and unsightly from a wooden spoon. Whatever it was, it was stubborn and that did not bode well.

"Your mother and I have come up with something a little special for tea," Aunt Vivien announced.

"Vivien says it's going to be a real treat," Mum said, glancing uneasily at the unfamiliar jars Aunt Vivien had piled up in front of the blender. She might as well have been announcing an incoming missile strike.

"I ate a big lunch," Greg blurted out, futilely.

"Nonsense!" Aunt Vivien declared. "Feed a cold, starve a fever! After a couple of healthy meals I'll have him fit as a fiddle."

She fixed a piercing glare on Greg, as though daring him to disagree.

"You two had better change and get cleaned up," Mum said. "Lewis, I've put Vivien in your room, so you have to double up with Greg. I've already moved some of your things."

Lewis sighed resignedly and slouched off upstairs after Greg. He risked a peek into his room as he passed and almost wept. A tower of luggage loomed over a wasteland of pink lace and delicate but tasteless ornaments, mostly statuettes of smug cats and simpering shepherdesses. Aunt Vivien had even gone so far as to bring her beloved Persian rug with its dizzying pattern of yellow and orange circles and triangles.

With a groan Lewis trailed despondently into the next room, where Greg was changing out of his school uniform while a song by his favourite metal band Rawkestra was blaring from the iPod. A rolled-up sleeping bag lay on the floor under the window where Lewis would be sleeping tonight.

Greg reached under the bed and plucked out two cans of cola. He tossed one to Lewis who caught it deftly. It was a gesture of solidarity in the face of disaster. They popped their cans in unison and drank as they got changed.

Lewis appreciated the effort Mum had put into tidying Greg's room so that he had some space to store his stuff, but he wished she had moved his computer in here. He'd been counting on finishing his current game of Spellshooter tonight before working on the files for his school project. He briefly considered sneaking into his room while Aunt Vivien was in the kitchen, but quickly dropped the idea. Aunt Vivien didn't tolerate her private space being intruded on, and she always knew. Maybe those prissy little shepherdesses kept a lookout for her, like guard dogs.

"Mum looks like she's spent the day being prodded in the back with a bayonet," said Lewis. "Why do you think she lets Aunt Vivien walk all over her like that? She doesn't act that way with Dad, let alone you and me."

"She used to be a nurse," Greg explained with a shrug. "She's obliged to take care of people, even Aunt Vivien."

"Remember the last time she cooked us a meal?" Lewis recalled gloomily.

"I remember liver, butter beans, spinach and some kind of sauce made out of gooseberries," Greg answered with a shudder. He cocked his head to one side in thought.

"Maybe I could work this cold up into something serious. I'd let you catch it," he added generously.

"Thanks for the offer," said Lewis, "but you can't trick your way out of Aunt Vivien. You might as well try to stop a tsunami by spitting at it."

"Hurry up, boys! We're just serving up!"

Aunt Vivien's cry shook them like an air-raid siren.

The boys headed downstairs to the dining room, dragging their feet as if they were encased in three tons of cement. The table had been laid with the best cutlery and there were paper napkins decorated with pictures of rabbits. As the boys sat down, Greg picked up his napkin and said, "Is it just me or do these rabbits look scared?"

Their eyes turned apprehensively as the kitchen door swung open with the creaking menace of the entrance to a crypt. A cloud of vegetable odours wafted out. Lewis half expected the wallpaper to peel off and slip to the floor, begging for mercy.

Aunt Vivien emerged in ghastly splendour with a glass casserole dish wrapped in a potholder in her upraised hands, looking for all the world like a pagan priestess presenting a sacrifice to some bloodthirsty god. Mum followed woodenly behind like she was in the grip of a voodoo spell.

"Just you wait, boys, we've a few more things still to

bring out of the kitchen," Aunt Vivien informed them ominously.

Greg and Lewis looked at each other aghast. If either of them had the nerve to turn and bolt for the door, the other would surely follow. As it was, they were as much prisoners as their mother.

"It's called Chicken Columbayo," Aunt Vivien announced proudly, setting the dish down in the centre of the table.

Inside, oddly shaped pieces of vegetable and blackened shreds of what had once been meat floated in a thick green liquid. A shower of white flakes had been liberally sprinkled over the surface. If they were lucky, it was only coconut.

Further dishes were laid out before them like forensic evidence from a toxic waste disaster. From previous experience they recognised Aunt Vivien's kidney beans in resin syrup and the notorious peppered potatoes, one nibble of which would have a professional fire-eater diving for the water jug.

"Adele has done a wonderful job, with just a teeny bit of supervision," Aunt Vivien confided as she commenced filling their plates with a generous helping from each dish.

"Well, it's mostly your work, Vivien," Mum said. "All I did was help." It was a weak stab at establishing her innocence.

Dinner commenced in a solemn silence, which Aunt Vivien took it upon herself to shatter brutally. It was her habit throughout any meal to keep up an unstoppable stream of gossip about people no one else had ever heard of or would ever wish to meet, and she did this while simultaneously gobbling up huge portions without pausing for breath.

Lewis tried to shut his ears to her talk of cousin this and Mrs So-and-so from somewhere or other. He poked a timid fork at his plate and speared what he believed to be a piece of chicken. Only DNA testing could establish it for sure. Slowly, fearfully, he raised it to his lips.

Later, laid out full length on the bed, Greg was so pale he could have been taken for a corpse if not for the groans issuing from his trembling lips. Lewis leaned out of the open window, heedless of the danger of falling. If he was going to throw up, he only hoped it would happen while the Larkins' dog was running past. That would pay it back for the time it had bowled him off his bike.

"What did she say that dessert was called again?" Greg asked without lifting his head.

"Scandinavian Ice Surprise," Lewis answered distantly.

"It was like eating cellophane. Come away from that window! You're not going to puke."

"I will if I'm lucky."

"That's it!" Greg exclaimed, sitting up abruptly. "That's what I was going to tell you before we spotted Aunt Vivien's car!"

"That feels like an awful long time ago," Lewis moaned.

Greg swung his legs over the bedside and stood up. "Stop malingering," he said, seizing Lewis by the collar and turning him around. "You can't let one bad meal finish you off."

"Up until a few seconds ago you were no picture of health yourself," Lewis accused.

"That was before I remembered my idea. I think I may have found a way around that test."

"You're not going to sleep with a pyramid under your bed again, are you? That didn't work last time."

"That was a valid experiment. No, this time you've given me the answer." He jabbed Lewis in the chest with his finger.

"Hey, I only suggested you study."

"Yes, you did, but I'm willing to overlook that."

He pulled a book from the pile Lewis had set neatly on the desk, knocking the rest of them to the floor. It was *The Folklore of Time* by Lucas Oberon Key. His eyes agleam with excitement, he flicked through it then flourished the open book triumphantly under Lewis' nose.

"Just take a look at *this*!"

3. RHYME WITHOUT REASON

At that moment there came a brisk knock at the door. Before they could say anything, it opened and Mum's face appeared through the gap. Greg shut the book and stuffed it under his arm.

"Can't you two come downstairs and be sociable for a while?" Mum demanded sharply.

The notion of deliberately spending time in Aunt Vivien's company left the boys too numb to respond.

"Vivien doesn't have any close family to fill her time, so she likes to be helpful," Mum said, piling on the pressure. "When she heard Dad was going away, she came straight here to help us out."

There was a brief pause when fate hung in the balance, then Greg brandished the book and said, "I've got to study. I've got a big test tomorrow."

Mum looked to Lewis for confirmation.

"It's true, Mum," Lewis said. "He has got a test."

"And what about you, young man?"

"I need to work on my school project," Lewis

answered, plucking up one of the books Greg had knocked to the floor.

Several seconds ticked by as Mum steamed in silence. "You'd better study," she said at last, "or you'll be dusting and carrying laundry for the rest of the year!"

Both boys nodded dumbly. They were well aware that Mum could make good on her threat.

She closed the door and her footsteps descended to where Aunt Viven waited. They could hear the distant buzz of a game show coming from the TV and Aunt Vivien's high-pitched laugh piercing the air like the sound of a drill.

"Boy, Mum's being a real ogre!" said Lewis.

"At least she let us stay out of the danger zone," Greg said.

"So what were you going to tell me that's so important?" Lewis asked, dropping the book onto Greg's desk, which was already halfway back to its usual state of disorganised clutter.

"Oh yes!" said Greg.

He darted a conspiratorial glance around the room before shutting the window, as though there might be someone outside listening. Lewis half expected him to search for hidden microphones. Greg opened the book on the folklore of time and presented it to Lewis with the victorious air of Sherlock Holmes exposing a murderer.

"What do you think of that?" he asked with upraised eyebrows.

Lewis read the page out loud.

"In the Orkney Islands of Scotland this rhyme, relating to a lost day of the week, was recorded by the Reverend Murdo Abercrombie in 1857. Its meaning, however, is obscure."

"So?"

"Read the rhyme, idiot!" Greg insisted.

Lewis read aloud in a long-suffering tone:

"The Lokiday Rhyme.
The day that was lost returns in time
If two will but recite this rhyme.
At Thorsday's end but say it fine,
Restore the day that once was mine."

"You see, it'll be a *lucky day*," said Greg. "And that's just what I need – luck."

"It says *Lokiday*, not *Luckyday*."

"So what? They spelled Thursday wrong too."

"Actually Thor was the Norse god of thunder," Lewis began. "Over the years the pronunciation—"

"Whatever! The main thing is that it's tonight, right? Thursday night."

Lewis treated his brother to as blank a look as he could muster.

"Don't you see?" Greg exclaimed impatiently. "That's all I need: just one day of good luck."

Lewis experienced a sinking feeling in his overfull stomach. "Is this going to be like the time you had us both dress in opposing primary colors so that when we stood together nobody would be able to see us?"

"It's not my fault that didn't work," Greg asserted bullishly. "Blame it on science."

"You don't get science from *The Amazing Book of Incredible Feats*," Lewis objected. "You have to join facts together and make something sensible out of them."

"Look, we say this rhyme and we'll have a lucky day," Greg persisted. "It's not brain surgery. Don't you want to be lucky?"

Lewis didn't have to think hard to come up with one area of his life where he'd like to be lucky.

"I suppose so," he agreed grudgingly. "But I don't think that's what it means. I think what it does is kind of conjure up this day that's disappeared. It brings it back."

"Okay, at worst, it's a whole extra day to study, and it might be lucky, too. Look, it says it takes two to make it work. So, are you in?"

"But does it make any sense that—"

"Switch off your brain for a second!" Greg commanded. "Your hair's starting to sizzle. Will you do it?"

Seeing that he had no choice, Lewis nodded.

"That's my boy!" Greg congratulated him with a hearty slap on the back.

This only confirmed to Lewis that he was making a big mistake. But unlike Greg's other schemes, if this didn't come off, then nothing would happen. Or would it?

Greg stretched out his forearm and checked his watch in a brisk, military fashion. "Just five hours to go. What'll we do until then?"

"You could always try breaking your golden rule and studying for the test."

"Studying? Don't be daft. I told you, tomorrow's going to be my lucky day."

Around ten thirty Mum found an excuse to unglue herself from Aunt Vivien. She came to Greg's bedroom door but was too disgusted with her sons to look in.

"Are you in bed yet?" she asked icily through the door.

"Yes, Mum!" they lied in chorus.

Mum was too dispirited by an evening in Aunt Vivien's company to press the point and slipped away to her bedroom before Aunt Vivien could call her back.

Lewis was in his pyjamas and climbing into the sleeping bag. He shut his eyes wearily, hoping that Greg would be so tired he'd forget all this nonsense about reciting the rhyme at midnight.

Lewis was having that dream where he turned up for school with no clothes on when a sharp poke in the ribs awoke him. "Come on, dozy, it's nearly time," he heard Greg say.

He struggled out of the sleeping bag and stifled a yawn.

Greg looked at his watch. "What time do you make it?"

Lewis looked blearily around him and picked his watch up from a nearby chair. "Eleven fifty-five."

Greg frowned. "I've got ten to midnight."

Lewis hated being forced out of a sound sleep and his tone was testy. "Yours hasn't worked right since that time you pretended to swallow it."

"I won the bet, didn't I?" Greg wrinkled his nose. "We need to be accurate if this is going to work. Hey, I know."

He stepped over to the window and yanked it open. "If we listen out we'll hear the town hall clock when it chimes midnight. As soon as it starts, we say the rhyme."

Lewis shivered as a cold breeze blew into the room.

"Fine, but once we're done, can we close the window and get some sleep?"

Greg frowned at him. "You might show a little enthusiasm. You know, you can't achieve anything in life if you won't believe in yourself."

Lewis' tolerance snapped. "This isn't about believing in myself. It's about you making me say this stupid rhyme because you're too lazy to do a little hard work."

Greg put his hands on his hips and regarded his brother through narrowed eyes. "We're both under a lot of stress right now, with Aunt Vivien and everything, so I'm going to assume you didn't mean that to sound as judgemental as it did."

Lewis sighed and glanced at his watch. "It's nearly time."

Greg picked up the book and flipped to the right page. Then he stood by the window with his ear cocked. When they heard the first chime of the town hall clock sounding in the distance, he pulled Lewis to his side.

"Okay, start reading."

"*The Lokiday—*"

"Not the title, you plank," Greg interrupted. "Just the rhyme. Start on the next chime."

They started together on the next stroke of twelve.

"*The day that was lost returns in time*
If two will but recite this rhyme."

Greg sped up, trying to complete the rhyme before

the clock finished striking. Lewis almost got tongue-tied trying to keep pace with him.

"*At Thorsday's end but say it fine,*

Restore the day that once was mine."

At the last word Greg shut the book with a flourish. "Close the window, will you? There's a draft."

Lewis pulled the window shut and yawned.

"Well, do you feel lucky?" he asked.

"It's not about *feeling* lucky," Greg retorted scornfully. "We need to test it scientifically." His gaze swept across the room. "I know."

He hauled open a drawer in his desk and raked through the assorted debris it contained. Some bottle tops and pencils fell out before he triumphantly lifted up a deck of cards. He thrust them at Lewis.

"Shuffle them and deal me five cards."

"Why?"

"It's a poker hand. If I get four aces or a full house, I'll know it worked."

Lewis opened his mouth to object then thought better of it. The sooner they got this over with, the better. He took the deck out of its box and shuffled it clumsily.

"Lewis, you're going to drop them all over the floor."

"I'm not a Las Vegas dealer, you know," grumbled Lewis.

He carefully dealt out five cards face down on the bed.

Greg snatched them up and pressed them to his chest as though afraid to look. Slowly he lowered them and looked. His face fell.

"These are total rubbish."

Lewis shrugged. "At least there wasn't any money riding on it."

Greg chewed his lip thoughtfully. "We should try it again, just to make sure."

Lewis heard his sleeping bag call and thought fast. The way things were going, he was either going to be dealing out cards all night or listening to Greg complain until dawn about his bad luck.

"It probably won't work till morning," he said. "That's when the day starts."

Greg considered this. "You may be right. Let's get some sleep. You look like you could use some."

"Right," Lewis said under his breath.

He burrowed as deep as he could into the sleeping bag and closed his eyes tightly. It was a good idea to doze off before Greg started snoring.

This time he had a dream in which Mum and Dad were sent abroad on a mission for MI5 and he and Greg had to go and live with Aunt Vivien. He was mumbling to himself about going out for a pizza when

34

he awoke with a shudder. The sun was shining through the curtains and the dream quickly vanished from his mind.

He didn't know yet that the day which lay ahead would be worse than any dream he had ever had.

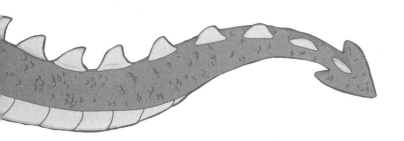

4. BREAKFAST WITH
A FLY

Mum's knock at the door was a lot heavier than usual. So heavy the door shook on its hinges.

"Rise and shine, boys! It's a school day!" she called.

Lewis heard her walk away and there was something unusual about that too.

"Do you hear that?" he asked.

"What?" Greg responded groggily.

"It sounds like Mum's dragging something across the floor behind her. A sack or something."

"Maybe it's Aunt Vivien's dead body. Why was she trying to smash the door down?"

"I've got no idea. Come on, let's try to get out of here before Aunt Vivien wakes up."

"Right, you go first." Greg yawned.

Lewis shambled off to the bathroom. He noticed with bleary eyes that the bathroom mirror now had an ebony frame carved with intertwining serpents. Returning to the bedroom, he became aware of how rough the carpet felt beneath his bare feet. He glanced down and saw that it was gone. In its place was a coarse mat woven from rushes or some such thing. He looked around for more strangeness and saw that the portrait of Grandad McBride that normally hung on the wall had been replaced with a painting of a grinning leprechaun.

The explanation was depressingly obvious, and it was just more bad news. Aunt Vivien suffered from occasional fits of redecorating. She had house-sat for them three years ago when they were on holiday in Canada, and they returned home to find a flea-infested moose head frowning down at them from above the TV set and strangely patterned Tibetan curtains hanging from most of the walls.

Dad had muttered that he would have felt more at home living in an igloo, and as soon as Aunt Vivien had completed her cheery farewells, all of her "little touches" were consigned to the darkest corner of the cellar.

It looked like she was at it again. She must have done it during the night while they were all asleep, as a surprise.

"Aunt Vivien's redecorating the house," Lewis reported gloomily when he returned to the bedroom.

"If I have to eat one more of her meals, I'll probably redecorate the house with the result," Greg said, dragging himself to his feet and shuffling off to the bathroom.

By the time he returned Lewis was fully dressed.

Greg scratched his head. "How can Mum let her get away with this?" he wondered as he threw on his clothes. "If she keeps on changing the house, maybe she can find some new people to come live here, too."

"That would suit me fine."

"We'd better eat breakfast before something happens to that as well."

They stepped out and padded past Lewis' room where they thought they could hear Aunt Vivien breathing softly. She rarely got up before ten o'clock and if she'd been up all night redecorating the house she might not get out of bed before noon.

Further gruesome signs of her handiwork greeted them downstairs. There was an enormous stuffed bat hanging on the wall. In the bookcase the encyclopedias and Dad's collection of spy novels had been replaced by rows of ancient volumes with mouldering covers.

Half the furniture had been replaced by crude tables and chairs carved from gnarled oak, many of which were decorated with vine patterns and gargoyle faces. Family photographs had been displaced by miniature paintings of spiders, wolves and odd half-human creatures Lewis couldn't even put a name to.

"This is so random!" he said, shaking his head.

"I think it's time we called in professional help," said Greg.

"You mean a psychiatrist?"

"I mean the SAS. Somebody's got to get rid of her and make the world safe for civilisation."

Lewis stopped short, scowling. "You know, she couldn't have done all this in one night. Not by herself. You don't suppose she made Mum help her, do you?"

"I wouldn't put anything past that woman."

They entered the dining room to find the table had been laid for breakfast. They sat down, casting their eyes uneasily over the pictures and ornaments, which had undergone the same sort of transformation as the rest of the house.

"I feel like I've moved into Frankenstein's castle," Lewis said.

Mum's voice came from the kitchen: "Breakfast will be right out!"

Greg lifted up his cereal spoon and made a face. All the cutlery had been replaced with crude, heavy items made from a dull, grey metal. "Aunt Vivien better not mess around with my breakfast," he groused. "Whatever you do, you don't interfere with a man's breakfast. It's the cornerstone of the whole day. If something goes wrong with breakfast, the knock on effect could spread to the whole country. It could devastate the economy. I've half a mind to call our MP, whoever he is."

At that moment the kitchen door opened and

something colossal came stomping out. It was about seven feet tall with green skin and tufts of black fur on the back of its ham-like hands. It had a big, knobbly face and nostrils almost as wide as its round, yellow eyes. A long, thick tail was dragging heavily across the floor behind it. It was wearing Mum's green summer dress and white apron.

"Just let me know if you want more," the monster offered, sounding just like Mum. It set a bowl down in front of each of them, then turned round and started back towards the kitchen.

The boys looked down, almost white with shock. Sitting in front of each of them was a bowl filled with a noxious yellow goo that looked like it had been scooped off the surface of a swamp. To add insult to injury, there was a fly floating on the top of Lewis' helping. He hoped for the fly's sake that it was dead.

He tried to say something to Greg, but all that came out was a choking noise.

The sound caused the green creature to halt at the kitchen door and lumber back to the table. It opened its wide gash of a mouth and Mum's voice came out. "Is everything all right, boys?"

They both stared at her, unable to speak, until a vexed frown began to form on that monstrous face.

Lewis' mouth had gone completely dry, but he

gathered the nerve to utter a single word. He pointed an unsteady finger at his bowl and whimpered, "Fly..."

The creature leaned over him, casting a vast shadow across the table. "Oh, don't worry about that," it said in Mum's sweetest voice.

The cavernous maw gaped open and a long, forked tongue whipped out to pluck the fly out of the gloop and pop it into the waiting mouth. The creature smacked its lips and lumbered back towards the kitchen.

"Now get on with your breakfast, boys," Mum's voice called. "You don't want to be late for school."

Greg won the race to the top of the stairs, but he had the good grace not to slam the bedroom door shut until Lewis had dived in after him. It only took them about half a minute to get the barricade up, and when they'd finished they slumped on the floor side by side, their backs resting against the heap of furniture and boxes now blocking the door.

"How long do you think we can stay in here?" Lewis asked once he'd caught his breath.

Greg's voice was shaky. "Until we starve." He drew the back of his hand across his mouth. "You know, this goes way beyond a spot of redecorating."

"Come on, you can't think Aunt Vivien's to blame for this."

"Why not? It's that muck she fed as last night. Look what it's done to Mum. It's only a matter of time before we start to mutate as well. Come to think of it, you already look kind of green."

Lewis ignored him and tiptoed over to the window. He gingerly eased aside the curtain and looked out over the back garden.

"What do you see?" Greg asked, sliding across the floor to his side.

"That well for one thing," Lewis answered. "Do you think Aunt Vivien dug that overnight?"

He pointed to a round well, which now occupied the centre of the garden. A bucket stood to one side of it with a rope tied to its handle.

Greg rubbed his eyes. "We're hallucinating," he said firmly. "She's drugged us. She put some kind of mushrooms in the food last night."

Lewis gave him a sceptical look. "It can't be a hallucination. We wouldn't both be seeing the same thing."

"Then it's a mirage," Greg insisted.

"You only get mirages in the desert. It's the sunlight refracting—"

Greg silenced him with an upraised hand. "Never mind. It's obvious what's going on. This is just a dream."

"You think we're both having the same dream?"

"Of course not, you idiot. You're not really here at all. You're just part of my dream."

"Then why are you bothering to talk to me if I'm not real?"

"I'm not talking to you. I'm only dreaming that I'm talking to you."

"Then why don't you go ahead and wake yourself up?"

"What, and lose my beauty sleep?"

"Won't that be better than being stuck in this nightmare?"

"You can't just wake yourself up," Greg objected. "If you could nobody would ever oversleep."

"It's got to be worth a try," Lewis said.

He walked over to the bulletin board and pulled a pin out of it, causing a newspaper clipping about a football match to flutter to the floor. "Here, stick this in your backside."

"What sort of a nutcase do you take me for?"

"It won't really hurt. It's only a dream, isn't it?"

"If it won't hurt, then stick it in *your* backside."

"How will that wake *you* up?"

"It probably won't," Greg agreed, "but right now I could use a good laugh."

"Take it from me, I'm really here and I'm awake. You're not dreaming me."

"So what's your theory?" Greg demanded.

Lewis backed away and sat down on the bed. "All I can think of is that this is Lokiday."

"Lucky, right. We have to eat slime for breakfast and Mum's turned into an orc."

"No, Lokiday," Lewis insisted, picking up *The Folklore Of Time*.

"You mean the rhyme?" Greg exclaimed, snatching the book from him. He flipped quickly to the page.

"I told you it was supposed to call up an extra day, not one that would be lucky for you." Lewis was too shaken to be smug. "Remember, it says, 'The day that was lost returns in time'. Suppose this is some sort of a lost day."

"You mean like the ones they rioted about back then?"

"Could be. Maybe even older than that."

"But if it's just another day, why is all this weird stuff going on?"

"Maybe if you give me the book I can find out."

Greg thrust the book at him and Lewis began to study it. He started with the Lokiday rhyme then flicked back and forth through the pages, searching for some further clue to what was happening.

"This book is a shambles!" he groaned. "There isn't even an index."

"If you hadn't brought that stupid book here in the first place," said Greg, "we wouldn't be in this mess."

"I never said, 'Hey, let's recite this rhyme at midnight.'"

"Oh, like you couldn't tell it was some kind of magic. Don't you pay any attention to what you're doing? Would you bring dynamite into the house and stick it in the microwave?"

"Magic?" Lewis repeated. "I suppose it is magic."

Greg stopped to look around him. "Why hasn't it changed my room?"

"Because it couldn't be in any worse shape than it is," Lewis responded bitterly.

"No, seriously. The rest of the house has changed, even the back garden."

Lewis drummed his fingers on an open page. "Maybe since we were making it happen, the spell couldn't affect us, or the place we were in, without undoing itself. It's like, if you're painting a floor, you can't paint the part you're standing on."

"How far do you think it goes?" Greg asked.

"What do you mean?"

Greg looked meaningfully towards the window. "Do you think it's just affected our house, or has it changed the whole town?"

Lewis looked outside. "You can't see much from here. The trees block the view."

"Do the trees look bigger to you?"

Lewis nodded reluctantly. He was about to speak when a flock of huge, black ravens erupted from the branches of the nearest tree with a raucous cry that sent him staggering backwards. They flapped up into the sky and wheeled away over their roof.

Before he could say anything, Lewis saw that Greg had put a finger to his mouth, signalling him to silence. Heavy footfalls were crossing the hall outside. Mum's voice sounded incongruously through the door.

"You didn't eat your breakfast," she called accusingly.

The boys looked at each other and Greg nudged Lewis to respond.

"We remembered some work we had to finish before school," he called back. "We had to come right up here and do it. Sorry... Mum," he added, trying to keep his voice from becoming a squeak.

There was a pause and they both eyed the doorknob anxiously.

"All right," Mum said. "But don't be late for school. Remember the fuss your dad made last time."

They heard her turn and lumber away, dragging her tail behind her. The boys let out a heartfelt sigh of relief.

"I've got an idea," Greg said.

He flicked on his radio, but all he could pick up

were waves of static. He switched it off and both of them reached for their phones. The message NO SIGNAL confirmed that they were completely cut off.

Greg tossed his phone on the bed. "So where does that leave us?"

"We could go out and explore," Lewis said. He did not sound keen.

"If we don't go to school soon, Mum's liable to smash the door down," Greg said.

"She could do it, too," Lewis added with a grimace.

"Look, Mum didn't seem to think there was anything strange about us. If we keep our cool, we can stroll around outside. Maybe we can find some other normal people."

"It would be a good idea to get out of here before Aunt Vivien wakes up," Lewis added. "If Mum's turned into a seven-foot tall green monster, what do you think *she's* turned into?"

"I don't even want to think about it."

"Come on, let's get the barricade down," Lewis said, taking hold of a chair leg. He saw that a pensive expression had spread over Greg's face. "What's the problem?"

"I was just wondering, how do you paint the piece of floor you're standing on?"

Lewis took a deep breath. "Could we worry about that some other time?"

Once they had dismantled the barricade Greg slowly opened the door. He looked back to see Lewis loading some books into his backpack.

"Come on!" he said.

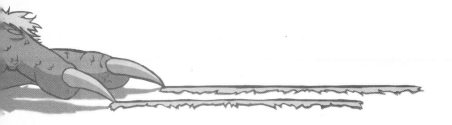

5. TOWN WITHOUT PITY

Lewis had been nurturing a slim hope that reality would reassert itself while they were hiding, but the leprechaun picture on the wall and the other unspeakable decorations were all still present. He sighed and steeled himself to follow Greg downstairs.

They were tiptoeing through the front hall when Mum appeared. Greg and Lewis grabbed hold of each other but managed not to scream.

"Since you didn't eat any breakfast," the seven-foot abomination said in Mum's most patient voice, "I've made you each a sandwich."

She handed them each something vaguely square shaped that was wrapped in a ragged cloth. Against his better judgement Lewis unwrapped the package and stared at the contents. Two mouldy slices of dry bread with shreds of some unidentifiable leaf drooping from the corners. Something was wriggling in the middle of the sandwich.

A fat, crimson spider poked its head out from

between the slices of bread then began to descend towards the floor on a slender thread. Lewis shook the sandwich rapidly and watched the spider fall.

Mum gave him a suspicious glare. "You haven't become a vegetarian have you?"

Lewis gulped. "I only eat spiders on Tuesday, Mum."

Upstairs a door opened and a chillingly familiar voice shouted out, "Do you have any herbal tea, Adele?"

Mum called back, "Yes, Vivien, I'll brew some nettles for you."

"I'll be right down!" Aunt Vivien trilled.

Lewis was rooted to the spot in horror until Greg shook him out of it.

"We've got to go, Mum!" Greg said urgently.

"Yes, right *now!*" Lewis blurted out.

They raced down the hallway, barely pausing to throw open the door before tumbling out into the street.

"That was close!" Greg gasped.

"Do you think it's okay to leave Mum alone with Aunt Vivien?" Lewis asked.

"In her present condition, I think she can take care of herself," Greg assured him.

A snuffling noise drew their attention to their left, where a large green dinosaur was curled up asleep on the driveway. There were no dice hanging over its nose, but there was no doubt that this slumbering beast had been Aunt Vivien's car.

All at once Lewis realised he was still holding the sandwich. Reflexively he flung it away.

Greg looked at his own package, holding it away from him at arm's length. Before he could decide what to do with it, a voice somewhere above them said, "Greg, you want that?"

They looked up.

Then they looked up some more.

The Chiz had to be at least twelve feet tall. He was covered in thick orange fur and his red beanie was so far off you'd have needed binoculars to see it properly. He'd have made a pretty fair Abominable Snowman.

Eventually Greg was able to say, "Hi, Chiz," without his voice breaking.

"Nice to see you, Chiz," Lewis added by way of support.

The Chiz was eyeing Greg's sandwich. A big red tongue slid out and moistened his thick lips.

"Oh, sure, Chiz, it's all yours," Greg said, offering the package.

The Chiz lifted it out of his hand with fingers the size of bananas. Without unwrapping it, he popped it straight into his mouth, chewed it three or four times and swallowed.

"Walk to school with you guys," Chiz rumbled. It sounded more like an edict than a suggestion.

"We've, uh..." Greg began.

"We need to go somewhere else first," Lewis finished for him.

"That's right, we've got an errand to run for Mum," Greg said.

"Can't miss school today, Greg. It's Lokiday."

"Right, Chiz."

Greg was just starting to walk away when one of the Chiz's immense, furry paws descended and clamped itself onto his shoulder. He squirmed manfully but could not get free. He felt himself being turned around and directed down the street towards school. It was either walk beside the Chiz or be dragged along, ruining the toes of his new trainers.

"Lokiday, eh. So I don't expect there'll be a test today, Chiz?"

The Chiz laughed like he'd made a really funny joke.

Lewis fidgeted nervously for a few seconds then he hurried after them. He was afraid that if he let Greg out of his sight, he would turn into something abominable as well.

"He seems even more spaced out than usual," Lewis observed to Greg in an undertone.

"The air's probably a little thin up there," Greg said.

Through the slatted fence of the Larkins' garden they caught an indistinct glimpse of something huge and hairy. It ripped a sapling out of the ground and tossed it high into the air. The animal looked like it wanted to play fetch, but they couldn't see whether there was anyone around with the strength or the courage to oblige. As they passed, it barked crazily, putting an extra spring in their step.

For the most part, the buildings along the street were only slightly altered. Some of them now had crooked chimneys giving off streamers of noxious green smoke, and they all looked a little dilapidated, as though they had aged overnight. Here and there a thatched roof or a turret had been added to a building, but the streets themselves appeared to follow the same pattern as before.

What was most noticeable was the complete lack of cars or bikes. There wasn't even the sound of an engine. Occasionally somebody would ride by on horseback or stroll past leading a mule. But there were bigger surprises than that in store in the transportation department.

On the spot where they usually passed Canny Dan's Snack Van, somebody had parked a wagon load of manure. It didn't smell any better. While they were pinching their noses, Darren Poole overtook them, not on his racing bike, but on a huge, loping lizard. Even with a mane of wild black hair and a set of fangs, Darren was still recognisable.

At the corner of Pipeland Road the lizard swerved aside to avoid a head-on crash with a colossal frog. The frog was hauling a carriage with Mr Arbuthnot, the bank manager, and his wife inside.

The boys spotted other familiar faces along the way, although on this particular day they were a little less familiar than usual. Lewis was relieved to see that not everyone had increased in size. The Brewster twins, for example, had become a pair of identical gnomes, with red beards and long, sharp noses. Susie Spinetti waved hello from across the street and seemed friendly enough, in spite of the fact she was dressed in goat skin and carrying a spear.

A hot-air balloon drifted overhead, manned by half a dozen rat-faced creatures who squealed in alarm as a dragon swooped out of the clouds and shot past them.

The Chiz had released his vice-like grip on Greg's shoulder by now, but neither brother felt inclined to wander far from him. The Chiz might have turned into a yeti, but he was still their friend, and provided a comforting sense of protection in the midst of the giant frogs and flying dragons. There could be little doubt left that Lokiday had transformed the whole population of

St Andrews and that Lewis and Greg were the only ones left who were aware that things had changed.

As they approached the school, they saw it was surrounded by a high spiked fence decorated with shields and animal skulls. The school building had sprouted two crenellated towers, and a row of ugly grey statues leered down from the roof. The din in the playground was almost deafening as leprechauns, dwarfs, elves, fairies, trolls, ogres and other misshapen creatures growled, squabbled, howled and sang.

"We're not seriously going in there, are we?" Lewis quailed.

"I don't know," Greg shrugged. "Frankly, it's not much worse than it is on a normal day."

Seeing them hesitate, the Chiz pressed his palms against their backs and herded them through the gate. They were plunged into the midst of the prancing, lumbering creatures who, the previous day, had been their schoolmates.

A figure in black armour came clanking out of the school and set about a crowd of gibbering gremlins with a whip, driving them ruthlessly indoors. The face below the upraised visor still resembled that of Mr Hawkins, the headmaster, even though it had taken on the appearance of a grinning skull.

Inside one of the new Gothic towers a bell tolled,

causing an immediate uproar. A set of double doors swung open like the entrance to a Transylvanian castle and the whole mob poured inside. Greg and Lewis were swept along helplessly, like fleas in bathwater spiralling down a plughole.

In the turmoil Lewis was buffeted this way and that. He realised to his dismay that he had lost sight of Greg and the Chiz. "Greg!" he called. But his voice was drowned in the hubbub.

Soon most of the pupils had found their way to a classroom and only the occasional scampering subhuman still whizzed past him, chattering excitedly to itself. Muffled roars, yelps and ragged choruses of disapproval could be heard booming behind the closed doors. Numbed by the excitement, Lewis discovered that he had made his way instinctively to his own classroom. He crouched low and sneaked up to the door. Raising his eyes over the edge of the glass window, he peeked inside.

A sphinx-like creature who had formerly been Mr Guthrie, the history teacher, was scrawling a series of bizarre hieroglyphics on the board and Lewis' classmates were copying them onto the slates they had on their desks. Lewis was almost tempted to take his place and try to blend in. But no, he had to find Greg and, if possible, work out a way to stop this nightmare.

He fell into a crouch and padded over to the stairs then sprinted up to Mrs Witherspoon's class where Greg would be. When he peeked through the glass his jaw dropped.

Greg's wrists were bound together with a length of rope that was looped over a hook on the wall, so that he dangled there with the toes of his trainers barely touching the floor. The imps, ogres and other mythological creatures who had been his classmates were lined up with a variety of weapons in their hands.

Off to one side stood Mrs Witherspoon. She looked like the witch from *The Wizard of Oz* – black dress and pointed hat, even the green skin. "You first, Malcolm," she said. "And try to do your best."

The satyr who had been Malcolm Strachan stepped forward on his goat's hooves and lifted the javelin he held in his right hand. His horns swayed from side to side while he tested the weight of the weapon.

"Remember," Mrs Witherspoon reminded him, "that you have to hit as close as you can without actually drawing blood. If Greg suffers a wound then you'll lose points."

Malcolm pawed the floor with one hoof then drew back his arm and threw. The javelin sliced through the air and stabbed into the wall under Greg's armpit.

"Cut it out, you creeps!" Greg burst out. There was an edge of panic in his voice. "This isn't funny!"

Lewis clenched his fists so tight his fingernails dug into his palms. Greg had said Mrs Witherspoon would like to use him for target practice, and now she was. She even looked like she was enjoying it.

The teacher waved forward Charlotte Gilmour, who was decked out in the garb of an ancient huntress, complete with bow and a quiver of arrows.

"You don't want to get on my bad side," Greg warned her, struggling with his bonds. "My dad plays golf with policemen and lawyers. Hundreds of them."

Charlotte fitted an arrow to her bow and raised it to fire. Before Lewis could make a move to interfere, she loosed off the shot. Greg yelped as the arrow thudded into the wall right by his left ear.

"Arthur, I believe you're next," said Mrs Witherspoon as she scribbled a note on the clipboard she was holding.

The Chiz lurched forward with a double-headed throwing axe in his paws. Lewis' heart sank and Greg tugged furiously at the rope. The Chiz couldn't hit the Great Wall of China if his nose was stuck to it, so if he was trying to miss, the result was certain doom for Greg.

"Chiz, maybe you'd like to pass on this," Greg

pleaded. Even from a distance Lewis could see the cold sweat dotting his brow.

"Quiet, Gregory, or I'll have to gag you!" Mrs Witherspoon snapped. The idea obviously appealed to her, as it had to Lewis on more than one occasion.

The Chiz lifted the axe clumsily and puffed his cheeks in and out as he always did when he was on the brink of wrecking something.

Lewis burst into the room with a desperate cry of, "Stop!"

All eyes turned to him, and thankfully the Chiz lowered his axe.

"What is the meaning of this?" Mrs Witherspoon demanded.

"You, uh, have to let him go," Lewis said unconvincingly.

"You are interrupting my class," said Mrs Witherspoon, bristling with displeasure.

Lewis swallowed hard. He had an awful premonition that he was about to be transformed into a frog. "He has to report to the headmaster," he improvised.

Seeing that Mrs Witherspoon was unswayed, Greg put on an imploring voice, "The headmaster! No, anything but that!"

"Mr Hawkins is tired of him messing around in

class," said Lewis. "I think he's going to boil him in oil or something."

"That's right, probably something worse," Greg added.

Mrs Witherspoon raised an intrigued eyebrow. "Well, under the circumstances, I suppose I shall have to let him go."

She pulled a jagged knife out of the folds of her black robe and cut Greg down. "But mind you don't miss your anatomy class!" she warned him.

"Right," Greg grunted warily.

He followed Lewis out of the room without breaking into a run, but only just.

Behind the door they heard Mrs Witherspoon call out, "Right, now we need a volunteer!"

"I thought school was rough before!" Greg exclaimed, rolling his eyes.

"At least there wasn't a test," said Lewis pointedly.

"That's funny," Greg frowned. "You should start a career as a comedian."

"If I hadn't come along when I did," Lewis reminded him, "they'd be peeling you off the wall with tweezers."

"I can't believe the Chiz was really going to throw that thing," Greg wondered. "After all the times I let him borrow my skateboard."

"You know, if you don't stop thanking me," Lewis cut in, "I'm going to start blushing."

Greg gave a terse nod and clapped his brother on the shoulder. "You did just fine. Really fine."

Lewis accepted that this was the best he was going to get. "Anytime," he said.

When they reached the main door, Greg asked, "Where are we going anyway?"

"Home," Lewis answered decisively. "That's where this whole mess started and that's where we'll find a way to undo it. If there is a way."

They had no sooner stepped outside than they were hailed by a gruff, overloud voice they recognised only too well. "Just the boys I've been looking for," it said like a judge passing sentence.

It was Mr Benson, the gym teacher. As a troll, he didn't look much different. His face was even rounder, his mouth wider, his belly bigger, and there was an orange tinge to his leathery skin, but other than that, he was still the same Mr Benson. And he smelled exactly the same: a malodorous blend of three-day-old sweat and cheap aftershave.

"I'm short a couple of players for the hogball team," he explained, tapping the pair of spiked clubs he had stuffed under his arm.

Lewis had never cared much for sports and the sort

of game this equipment implied made him go pale. "Hogball?" he repeated limply.

"Two of the team went down injured in the last game," Mr Benson growled. "Worse than that, somebody fell on the hog and killed it."

"We'd love to help out, but we can't," Greg said.

"Why not?" the gym teacher challenged.

"Because..." Greg said vaguely. He gave Lewis a nudge then saw that his younger brother was too distressed by the prospect of contact sports to be any help.

"Because I've got to get him home. He's having a seizure," Greg blurted out.

He stared expectantly at Lewis. So did Mr Benson.

Lewis couldn't think how to fake a seizure, so, to his own surprise, he started to bark. Greg smiled weakly and patted him on the back.

Mr Benson shook his head in disgust. "There's too much of this going on," he complained. "If you boys spent more time on the sports field and less time messing around with magic, we wouldn't have this kind of trouble."

He stomped into the school in search of alternative victims.

Greg breathed a sigh of relief. "It was my turn to save you," he said. He grabbed Lewis by the arm and dragged him towards the gate. "Come on. It's time you got us out of this."

As soon as they cleared the schoolyard they broke into a trot, hoping to avoid further encounters with giants, trolls or any other sort of monster. They were scarcely halfway home when they were ambushed – again.

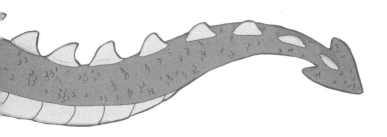

6. NO FUN WITH
A FAIRY

One second the pavement was empty. The next, there was a flash that made them grab each other for protection.

Lindsay was floating in the air in front of them. She was a good metre off the ground, supported evidently by the large butterfly wings fluttering at her back. Her hair glinted like gold and she wore a short, gossamer gown. Her glasses were studded with what looked like real diamonds.

"Where did you come from?" Greg cried. He could hardly believe that with all the other things that had gone wrong, Lindsay had ambushed them two days running. This time she really had appeared out of thin air.

Lindsay made a huffy face. "I have a seat by the window and I saw you running off. I thought there might be some fun going on, so I left when Mr Guthrie wasn't looking. I mean, who ever died from not learning hieroglyphics?"

"Nobody yet!" Greg said pointedly.

"Greg, be nice to her," Lewis whispered, pulling his brother aside. "We could use her help."

"To do what? Style our hair?"

"Look, she's harmless. If we let her tag along, maybe she knows something that could help us out."

Greg looked dubious, but grudgingly nodded. He turned to Lindsay with a smile that wouldn't have fooled anyone but her.

"Lindsay, you look nice. Your outfit, your hair, your, uh... wings. Nice."

Lindsay beamed radiantly for a second then vanished. Greg let out a yelp when she reappeared only centimetres from his face.

"Sorry, Greg," Lindsay apologised, clasping her hands together and lowering her eyes. "Sometimes I just twinkle without meaning to."

Greg tried to stop himself making a sickly face. "*Twinkle?*"

Lindsay nodded shyly. "That's what we fairies call it."

"It's a good trick, Lindsay," said Lewis.

"Oh, it's something any fairy can do," Lindsay responded modestly.

"You see," Lewis said into Greg's ear, "she can *twinkle!*"

"Yes, that's going to be a big help," Greg answered sceptically.

"So why did you run out of school?" Lindsay asked.

"It's Lokiday," Lewis said nonchalantly, "so we thought we'd take the rest of the day off."

"We're going to go home and relax," said Greg, "take a nap, watch some TV."

"What's teevee?" Lindsay asked naively.

"You know, where you watch those singing shows and that thing about the models," said Lewis.

Lindsay gave him a blank stare.

"Never mind," Lewis said.

A thoughtful look came across his face as they carried on down the street with Lindsay hovering above them. "Lindsay, do you remember when we met around here yesterday?"

"What's yesterday?" Lindsay asked unconcernedly. She was still looking at Greg.

"The day before today," Lewis said.

"And today's Lokiday," Lindsay said.

"Right," Lewis agreed.

"So what do you want to know?"

"It was your idea to let her tag along," Greg muttered.

"The spell's clouded her mind," Lewis surmised.

"She had a head start on that."

They walked along to the accompaniment of Lindsay's chatter about the latest fairy fashions, gossip about what some of the elves at school were up to and her mum's new crystal ball.

Greg tried to ignore her. "Have you come up with a plan yet other than letting Tinkerbell follow us around?" he demanded of Lewis.

Lewis hummed uncertainly. "I've got lots of information about time stored on my computer as part of my project. If I could get to it, maybe it could help us sort things out."

"Why should your computer be there? It's probably turned into a toadstool or something."

"Not everything's changed. Your room's stayed the same and mine's right next door. Even downstairs some of the furniture's the same. It's worth a try, isn't it?"

Greg glanced up at Lindsay and said, "Anything's worth a try."

When they turned the corner into Bannock Street, Greg stuck out an arm to stop Lewis going any further. Parked in front of their house was a coach painted red and green led by two tethered goats. As big as horses, they were busily devouring the front hedge.

In the driver's seat sat a tall figure in a leather coat with a long, sharp face that looked like it was made of ice. He wiped away a drip from his icicle of a nose and made a half-hearted effort to pull the goats away from the bushes.

"What's that doing there?" Lewis asked.

"I'll bet it's got something to do with Aunt Vivien," Greg groaned.

Lindsay gaped at the carriage. "Isn't that the cutest thing! Could you take me for a ride in it?"

"It's not ours, Lindsay," Lewis explained. "We don't know who it belongs to."

"Best not to find out," Greg said. "The fewer weirdos we run into, the better."

They ducked and took a roundabout route to their back garden. They slipped stealthily through the gate and wove a cautious path around the well that had appeared that morning.

Lindsay bobbed excitedly up and down in the air in front of them. "Is this some kind of a game we're playing?" she asked.

"Yes, it's loads of fun," Greg agreed, signalling her to shut up.

"Ooh, a Lokiday prank!" Lindsay squeaked. "Can I help?"

Greg was starting to seethe. "It would be a big help if you got—"

"See that window up there, Lindsay?" Lewis interrupted in the nick of time. He was pointing to his bedroom window. "Could you fly up there and see if anybody's inside?"

"Is this part of the prank?" she asked brightly.

Lewis nodded.

"Yes, it's hilarious," Greg said. "Now will you fly up there?"

Lindsay flitted up to the window and peered inside.

"There's nobody there," she said just loud enough for the boys to hear.

"Is my computer there?" Lewis asked eagerly.

Lindsay frowned, her little nose wrinkling under her glasses. "What's a computer?"

"Well, it's got a glass screen and it can answer questions."

Lindsay peered into the room. "Yes, it's there," she reported, looking pleased.

"Going in through the door is too risky," Greg grimaced. "We'll have to climb up the drainpipe."

"Lindsay can fly," Lewis said thoughtfully. "Maybe she could carry us up there one at a time."

Greg's face took on an instantaneous look of horror. He clamped a hand over his brother's mouth before Lindsay could hear him, and repeated with grim determination, "We'll have to climb up the drainpipe."

Lewis looked up. "Lindsay, could you twinkle inside and open the window please?"

"Yes, if that's what you and *Greg* want."

"It's what we both want," Greg confirmed. He made a face at her as she blinked out of view.

Marching up to the drainpipe, he took a firm grip with both hands and began hauling himself up. Luckily there were enough cracks in the worn brickwork to provide footholds.

By the time he reached the top Lindsay had opened the window and was standing back to leave him space. He clambered in and fell to the floor in an ungainly fashion.

Lewis came puffing over the window ledge and lowered himself to the floor one foot at a time. He could see at once that the room had changed, just like the rest of the house. There were stone statues of dragons and gargoyles dotted about the place, garish hangings on the walls, and the air was so thick with incense it was stifling.

Aunt Vivien's ghastly Persian rug was one of the things that still looked the same, but there was no sign of Lewis' computer.

"Where's the computer, Lindsay?" he asked.

Lindsay pointed to the mirror hanging on the wall. "It's not what I'd call it, but why quibble."

"That's not a computer," Lewis told her, aghast.

"It has a glass screen and it answers questions," Lindsay insisted. She sounded a little hurt.

"And you told me what a big help she'd be," Greg reminded Lewis.

Lindsay pouted. A tiny tear sprang to her eye and she disappeared.

"Now look what you've done!" Lewis accused.

"Big deal. She just made us bash our knees in for nothing."

"Maybe not. She said it answers questions."

Understanding dawned on Greg's face. "You mean it's a magic mirror, like in a fairy tale."

"It makes sense, I suppose. But how do we start it up?"

"That's simple," Greg told him confidently. "Have you never seen *Snow White*?"

He walked up to the mirror and saw that instead of his reflection, the glass was filled with a swirling mist. He cleared his throat and spoke in a commanding voice. "Mirror, mirror on the wall, who is the fairest of them all?"

The twisting clouds rapidly formed an exotic face. It wore a red turban and had a long, aristocratic nose. Its large green eyes gazed out of the glass in a bored fashion and its forked beard twitched as it spoke.

"What sort of a question is that? You boys aren't much of a beauty contest."

Greg took an involuntary step backwards then

steadied himself. "Forget about the beauty stuff," he said. "That was just to get your attention."

The Face yawned. "So?"

Greg paused and thought for a moment. "It probably only answers to rhymes."

"Why would you think that?" Lewis objected, but Greg waved him to silence.

"Mirror, mirror on the wall, open up and tell us all," Greg intoned.

The Face gazed back scornfully. "You didn't say the magic word."

"Tell us all, *please*," Greg said in a long-suffering tone.

The Face looked away and its eyebrows did a fair imitation of a pair of arms being crossed.

"What's the problem?" Greg demanded. "I said what he wanted."

"That's not what he wants," said Lewis. "Remember he's kind of like a computer. He wants the password."

The Face quirked an eyebrow. "Yes, the password," it agreed superciliously.

"Go ahead and give it to him then," Greg said.

Lewis cast an embarrassed sidelong glance at his brother. "Could you maybe step outside for a second?"

"Get on with it," said Greg. "Give him the password."

Lewis leaned as close to the mirror as he could and whispered, "Lindsay."

"Lindsay?" Greg repeated in a voice dripping with scorn. "That is *tragic!*"

"Don't..." Lewis began, then groped helplessly for the next word. "Just don't."

"If you're quite finished," the Face piped up.

"Sorry about that," Lewis told it sheepishly.

"Don't apologise to me," the Face said. "I'm your servant, remember."

"So serve us then," Greg demanded, placing his fists on his hips.

"Who asked you to stick your nose in?" said the Face. "The little fellow's the boss. He's the one who said the magic word."

Lewis bristled. "What do you mean 'little'?"

"Forgive me, mountainous one," the Face said in an off-handed manner. "What is your request?"

"Well, tell us what's going on."

The Face grimaced. "I hate to carp, but do you think you could be a shade more specific?"

"Well, yesterday, there were cars, TVs and computers. Today there are monsters, fairies and magic mirrors."

"And Mum is an ogre," Greg added.

"I don't know what you're talking about," said the Face.

"We said a rhyme and everything changed," Lewis explained.

The Face made a quizzical expression. "I'm not aware of any change, O baffling one."

"No, that's because you're part of it," said Lewis. "The whole of reality has been altered."

The Face let out a low whistle. "That's too heavy for me. You need to consult the Fount of All Knowledge."

"What is that?" Greg demanded.

The Face contorted in thought. "I don't know. It just sort of popped into my..." its eyes rolled around searchingly, "head."

"You mean you're giving us advice that you don't understand yourself," Greg said irritably.

"You have a gift for the obvious," said the Face. "Why should I need to understand it? I'm not the one with the problem."

Greg turned assertively on his brother. "Okay, what's this Fount of All Knowledge?"

Lewis lowered his eyes. "I don't know."

Greg chewed his lower lip then stabbed a finger decisively in the air. "The drinking fountain in Kinburn Park!"

"I don't think it's that kind of fount."

"Well, at least I have a suggestion."

"Such as it is," the Face put in.

"It's not like you've been a big help, Glasshead," Greg retorted.

The Face ignored him and addressed Lewis with exaggerated politeness. "If you are done with me, O unfortunate sibling, I shall return to the nothingness from which I came. And with some relief, I might add."

So saying, the Face dissolved into the swirling mist that covered the mirror's surface. Greg made an unpleasant gesture at the glass.

"Just a moment," they heard a voice call from outside the room. "I must fetch my coat first."

It was Aunt Vivien. There was no mistaking that piercing tone and they could hear her footsteps climbing the stairs towards them.

"We need to hide!" Lewis gasped in sudden panic.

"No time," Greg said grimly. "Out the window!"

"We'll break our necks," Lewis objected.

"Slide over and hang on with your fingers, then let go," Greg told him. "It's not that big a drop. Now do it!"

The prospect of confronting a monster version of Aunt Vivien was enough to snap Lewis into action. He swung himself over the window ledge and slipped down till he was only just hanging on, with his legs dangling over the back garden.

He wasn't inclined to let go, but he was delaying Greg's escape by hanging on. He relaxed his grip and slid down the wall, the rough brickwork tearing up the front of his jumper. When he hit the ground his legs folded up and he collapsed into a ball. He lay there checking for broken bones until he was sure he wasn't injured.

He was about to get up when he noticed that he was staring at the toes of a pair of black boots. He followed them up a pair of long legs to where a tall, blonde woman stood over him. She was wearing chainmail and a round helmet with wings on the sides.

"So I find you crawling in the grass like a worm, just as should be expected," she announced grandly, as though she were performing a scene out of an opera. She seized the hilt of the sword that hung at her side and pulled it from its sheath. "It's time you were dealt with."

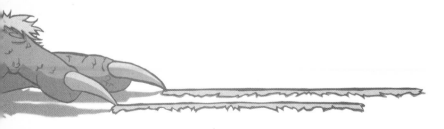

7. ONE COIN IN THE FOUNTAIN

It was at that moment that Greg dropped from the window and landed squarely on top of the woman. They tumbled to the ground in a tangle of limbs and chainmail. Greg was the first to crawl dazedly out of the mess.

Lewis grabbed his arm and hauled him to his feet. "Anything broken?" he demanded.

"No, I'm fine."

"Good. Let's get out of here."

Lewis set off at a run, dragging Greg bemusedly behind him.

"Who is she?" Greg asked.

"A Valkyrie, I think. Never mind that right now. We have to get away."

As they rushed out of the gate, he glanced back and saw the warrior woman rise to her feet. Instead of chasing them, she stuck two fingers in her mouth and let out a sharp whistle.

Her summons was answered by the weirdest

thing they had yet seen on a day when the weirdness factor was already in the high nineties. It looked like a modern sculpture of a horse made out of scrap metal with two motorcycle wheels instead of legs. It came racing round the corner of the house with a high-pitched whinny and a hiss of pistons. Its eyes glowed red and steam puffed from its flared metal nostrils.

"This doesn't look good," Greg observed, lengthening his stride so that Lewis no longer needed to pull him along.

Sprinting down Spottiswood Gardens, they looked back to see the Valkyrie rounding the corner on her metal steed.

Lewis followed Greg's lead and raced down to Broomfaulds, where they ducked behind a stone tomb graven with images of knights and monsters. Yesterday it had been a bus shelter.

The Valkyrie came roaring past, too caught up in her own rage to notice them crouching there in the shadows. As she disappeared into the distance, the boys slumped against the tomb and gasped in relief.

"Now can you tell me who your girlfriend is?" Greg asked.

"I think she's a Valkyrie. They were warrior maidens in Norse mythology. They gathered up the souls of dead warriors and took them to Valhalla where they'd feast for all eternity."

"The feasting part sounds all right, but what does she want with us? We're not dead yet."

"I don't know," Lewis answered with a weary shake of the head. "This whole thing just gets worse and worse."

Greg sensed the despair in his brother's voice. He put his hand on Lewis' shoulder. "The fountain in Kinburn Park," he said confidently. "We'll find the answer there. Trust me."

Lewis was unconvinced, but too exhausted to argue. Besides, he had nothing better to offer.

Greg helped him to his feet and they shuffled off in the direction of the park, casting wary glances about them the whole way. At one point they saw a Valkyrie speeding down Canongate Road while they skulked behind a bush of spiky thorns with huge orange berries.

"She doesn't give up easily, does she?" Greg said.

They entered the park and passed some fairies who were dancing on the grass. Lewis checked that Lindsay wasn't amongst them. He hoped she wasn't still cross with them.

Greg led the way with groundless confidence, having convinced himself that he was in control of the situation. The bowling lawn and putting green had been submerged by a lake, where large and unsettling shapes moved vaguely beneath the water. They gave this a wide berth and warily circled an adventure playground filled with spikes, blades and iron balls. A few goblins were capering there without coming to any apparent harm.

The humble drinking fountain had been transformed into a circular pool, in the middle of which was a marble monument in the shape of a sea god, half man, half fish. He grasped a trident in his right hand and a stream of water gushed from his open mouth.

"Okay, so it's a fountain," said Lewis. "But how does that help us?"

"You know, you could be a bit more supportive," Greg told him. "I'm starting to get into this stuff."

"Suppose this is the Fount of All Knowledge then," Lewis conceded. "What do you do with it?"

"It's a fountain, you idiot. You toss a coin in."

Greg reached into his pocket and pulled out a pound coin. He stared at it for a second then put it back and fished out a ten pence piece instead.

"If it doesn't work, there's no sense throwing money away," he explained.

He flipped the coin into the air and watched it plop into the fountain. He stared fixedly at the spot where it had sunk. In spite of his doubts, Lewis found himself also watching expectantly.

For a while nothing happened. Then, just as Lewis was about to suggest they leave, the waters around the fountain began to bubble.

They took a startled step backwards, but before they could get safely out of the way, a long, serpent shape, as thick as a tree trunk, shot straight up out of the bubbles. Three metres above their heads, a lizard-like face fixed them with a hostile gaze.

"You're a long way from Loch Ness," Greg gasped.

The creature spat something out then flopped back into the fountain, dashing water all over them and soaking their clothes. The coin came twirling out of the air and dropped at Greg's feet with a tiny clink.

"Well, so much for that idea," he said, pushing his wet hair back out of his face and retrieving the coin.

"Maybe if you weren't such a cheapskate..." Lewis began.

He was silenced by the look on his brother's face. Greg was staring in the direction of the playground and when he turned to look, Lewis saw the reason for his alarm.

The Valkyrie had burst out of the trees and was bearing down on them. She pulled back on the reins and halted her snorting mount only a few metres away from them. She glowered, the way you look at a bug just before you step on it.

"I don't know who you are," Greg told her bullishly, "but you're getting to be a real pain in the neck."

Lewis made a feeble effort to pull him back as the woman raised an imperious eyebrow. "I am Shona, chief of the Valkyries," she declared grandly.

"Shona?" Lewis repeated. He peered at her. "Hang on, I recognise you. You're Shona Gilhooley, the woman that runs the aerobics class Mum goes to on Tuesday night."

The Valkyrie drew her sword. "You mock me at your peril, whelp! I know nothing of this *aerobics class* you speak of."

"Look, we're not going any place with you," said Greg, "feasting or no feasting."

"Cease your prattling, you witless fool," said the Valkyrie, pointing the blade directly at him. "You cannot outrun my roadsteed. You will come with me now, either as my prisoners or as trophies."

"Come with you where?" Lewis asked.

"My master demands your presence," Shona Gilhooley answered, edging her mount closer. Its eyes narrowed and a thin sliver of steam drifted from its snout.

"Look, if Mr Hawkins sent you," said Lewis, "tell him we'll get back to school as soon as we can."

"Right," Greg agreed, "you can push off and leave us in peace."

The Valkyrie laughed a rich, lingering laugh.

"She's not talking about Mr Hawkins," Greg surmised.

"Good guess," Lewis agreed.

"Yonder come my sisters," Shona announced.

The boys looked around and saw five more Valkyries closing in on them from different directions, all riding roadsteeds.

"You've got the wrong guys," Greg said desperately. "You're looking for Hansel and Gretel, or the Babes in the Wood, or the Brothers Grimm."

"Enough!" the Valkyrie snapped. She leaned forward to take a swipe at Greg with her upraised blade, coaxing her mount forward as she did so.

At that precise moment Lindsay materialised in midair right in front of her. The roadsteed pulled up short and Lindsay reached out and yanked the Valkyrie's helmet down over her eyes.

"Run!" she urged the brothers, swooping along behind them as they took to their heels.

They heard the engine roar of the other Valkyries revving their roadsteeds for the chase. The boys dashed into the trees, only pausing for breath once their pursuers were out of sight.

"Thanks, Lindsay," Lewis said. "You're a life saver."

"Yes, thanks," Greg mumbled.

"You weren't very nice to me, Greg," Lindsay said

huffily, "but I still wasn't about to let those Amazons get their hands on you."

"Valkyries, actually," said Lewis, pointing behind them through the trees to where two of the warrior women were riding in their direction.

"Look out!" Lindsay squeaked.

Another Valkyrie erupted from the greenery, scattering the three of them as her mount reared up, its eyes ablaze. Lindsay shot straight up in the air while the boys split off to the left, racing through the foliage for all they were worth.

Luckily the transformed park was thickly wooded, making it difficult for the Valkyries to manoeuvre their roadsteeds. The boys zigzagged right and left, crouching low to make themselves less visible.

All at once Lewis realised he had lost sight of Greg again. He groaned, frantically imagining what sort of a scrape his brother was going to get himself into this time. Something about what had happened to Greg at school was nagging at the back of his mind, like an itch he couldn't reach to scratch.

Before he could give it any more thought, he heard someone hiss at him. Greg was scrunched down in the bushes to his right, waving him over.

He scurried to his brother's side and squatted down next to him. "What happened to Lindsay?" he asked.

"Like it matters!" Greg snorted.

"She did save us just now," Lewis reminded him sharply.

Greg could see he was upset and spoke in a conciliatory tone. "I just meant she can always *twinkle* out of trouble."

Lewis harrumphed to show he was still irked with him.

"Never mind about that just now," Greg said. "We need a place to hide and there it is."

He pointed through the bushes at a long wooden building on the edge of the lake.

"It looks like a boathouse," said Lewis.

"It's only a quick dash away," said Greg. "We can hole up there till things quieten down."

"It sounds good to me."

"Right, when I go, you stick with me," Greg instructed.

He craned his neck for a cautious look around. They could hear the roar of the roadsteeds' engines, but none of them were visible.

Greg gave his brother a warning nod, then leaped out of the bushes to sprint across the open ground. Lewis followed fast and it took only seconds for them to reach the boathouse. Greg wrenched open the door and bundled Lewis inside.

There was just one boat, but it was about five metres

long and its prow was decorated with a dragon's head carved out of wood.

"What is this, a Viking theme park?" Lewis asked.

"Never mind that," Greg told him as he pulled the door shut. "Just stay out of sight and keep quiet."

They crouched by the door where Greg could peek out through a knothole. He saw one of the Valkyries wheel past no more than a few metres away. She reined in her mount and looked over at the boathouse.

"One of them's headed this way," he said. "We've got to hide."

"Where?" Lewis gasped, staring around helplessly. Then he spotted a pile of canvas lying at the bottom of the boat. "We can hide under that," he said, pointing.

Without another word they jumped into the boat and wriggled under the canvas. "Your leg's sticking out!" Greg whispered urgently.

Lewis quickly pulled his leg in and tugged the canvas down to conceal himself. They were shrouded in darkness and silence, broken only by the exaggerated sound of their own breathing. Then the boathouse door was kicked open and Lewis heard a sword rasping from its sheath.

He listened to the Valkyrie pace the landing then stop. The toe of her boot tapped impatiently. The brothers held their breath, trying not to make the slightest movement that might give them away.

Finally the Valkyrie snarled a Germanic curse and marched out, slamming the door behind her.

Greg and Lewis crawled out from under the canvas.

"That was close!" Lewis gasped, gratefully breathing in the fresh air.

A loud snort suddenly drew their eyes to the boat's dragon prow in time to see its eyes open. The prow stretched its neck as if to untangle a kink, then twisted around to look at them.

The boys jumped out and stood in astonishment while the dragon's head blinked at them.

"What are you two doing here?" it asked in a deep, rough voice. "Don't you know this is my nap time? Don't you know I need my sleep? Is this any kind of time to come looking for a boat ride? What do they teach kids these days?"

"Shhh!" Greg told it.

The dragon prow raised its eyebrows. "Son, you've got a communication problem. I asked you a question and all you can do is hiss."

"Please be quiet!" Lewis pleaded.

The dragon head twisted about on its wooden neck. "I say, am I missing something here? I'm the one that got woken up and you're trying to hush me. It makes no sense, boy. There's no reason to it. If you're here for a boat ride, just come out with it." It paused to look back and forth between them. "Nod if any of this is sinking in."

"We don't need a boat ride," Greg told it. "We're just chilling."

"This is a boathouse, boy, not an icehouse," the dragon head told him. "Do you see any ice here? No, because there isn't any. You come to a boathouse to use a boat, longship that is. Which I am."

The dragon prow ignored Lewis' desperate efforts to signal him to silence. Finally it said, "Stop waving your arms around, boy. You look like a windmill."

"Look, we don't need a boat," Greg said. "But I hear there are some Vikings dropping by later to pillage the picnic area. Maybe you should rest up in case they need a quick getaway."

"Hmm..." the dragon said. "I could use a tad more shuteye if it's going to be a busy day. Thanks for the tip-off, son. You and your gobby friend be sure to wake me if those Vikings show up."

The dragon head slowly shut its wooden eyes and pretty soon it looked completely lifeless again.

"We'd better hide out here until the coast is clear," said Greg. "It should be safe, as long as big mouth doesn't start sounding off again."

"Let's take a seat behind that barrel over there," Lewis suggested.

He hauled *The Folklore of Time* out of his backpack and tried to read through it in an orderly manner. It wasn't easy. It kept jumping from one topic to another in a series of badly organised chapters, most of which were little more than a page in length.

One was on various ways in which time had been measured – hourglasses, marked candles, sundials and the like – another was on the Inca calendar, and another was about unlucky days like Friday the thirteenth. Nowhere was there any further mention of Lokiday.

Still, Lewis persevered in the hope that he would find a way out of their predicament. There was always a chance that the Fount of All Knowledge the mirror had directed him to might be this book, but the more he read the more he doubted it.

Looking up from a chapter on pagan festivals, he noticed that Greg had dozed off – just switched off all the weirdness so that it wouldn't interfere with today's quota of loafing. At least, Lewis reflected, that meant he could read in peace.

By the time he'd finished with the book, his back was stiff and aching. He gave Greg a poke with his elbow.

"I think it's safe now."

Greg rubbed his eyes and stretched his arms. "I've been giving this situation some thought," he announced.

"In between snores, I suppose."

Greg was too busy being pleased with himself to take any notice of his brother's sarcasm. "Why do we need to leave here at all?"

"Well, for one thing, the boat might wake up."

"Apart from that. This day we've conjured up, it's just a day, right?"

"What are you on about?"

"Look, if we hide out here till the morning, the day will be over. It'll be Friday and everything will be back to normal."

"Maybe," Lewis conceded. He looked around. "This isn't exactly a comfy place to stay holed up."

"It's not for long," Greg assured him, glancing at his watch. "What time do you make it? I think I'm running slow."

Lewis sighed, wondering if Greg would ever stop fooling around with his watch and let it run properly. He checked his own watch. "Eleven thirty."

"Is that right?" Greg sounded puzzled. "How long have we been here?"

"It feels like an hour at least, but..."

"But what?"

Lewis was staring at his digital watch. When he started reading the book it had read 11:30:56. It still read 11:30:56. Even as he stared at it, it didn't change.

Greg craned over to take a look. "It's broken," he concluded. "You should learn to take better care of it."

"Well, why don't you check your watch?"

Greg lifted his wrist and looked at his own watch again. It was still five minutes behind Lewis', but he had the same problem. The display wasn't changing. Lewis grabbed him by the arm and looked back and forth between the two watches.

"Is this another thing that's been messed up by that stupid rhyme?" Greg asked grumpily.

Lewis' face screwed up in thought. "It was working fine before. This is something new. If our watches were affected by the Lokiday spell, they would have gone wrong the same time as everything else changed."

He shot to his feet, dashed to the door, and took a look outside. "I swear the sun hasn't moved since we ducked in here," he said.

Greg joined him and squinted at the sky. "So what's going on?"

"I haven't a clue. But I think we have to find the Fount of All Knowledge."

"What's your rush?" said Greg with a shrug. "We've got all the time in the world, by the looks of it."

"That's just the trouble," said Lewis. "Don't you see? If time's stopped dead, it's going to be Lokiday forever."

8. ONE SAGE IN A SPHERE

"You mean Mum will be an ogre forever and I'll keep getting used for target practice?" Greg moaned.

Lewis didn't respond. Greg's words had reminded him of something that had been gnawing at him for a while now, and at last he began to understand what it was. His face suddenly brightened.

"That's it!" he exclaimed.

"That's what?"

"The Fount of All Knowledge. Don't you see?"

Greg folded his arms and looked at Lewis as though he were dribbling all over his shirt. "Whatever it is, I don't see it, hear it or smell it."

"Look, yesterday you said Mrs Witherspoon would like to use you for target practice."

"And I was right!"

"And last night I said Mum was being a real ogre."

Greg's brow furrowed. "You mean *we're* doing all this?"

"Not exactly," said Lewis. "The spell's working on its

own, but some of our thoughts have influenced it. You always complain how Lindsay pops up out of nowhere, and now she does it for real."

"If she's turned into a fairy because of something I said about her, then she got off lucky. I've said a lot worse."

"I know," Lewis retorted accusingly. "But we won't bother about that right now."

Greg returned to the main point. "But the rest of the town, that's got nothing to do with us, right? I've never even heard of a Valkyrie."

"Well, we did recite the rhyme, but it can't all have been guided by us. Although a lot of things have changed in ways that fit our ideas about them."

Greg made a sickly face. "If that's true, what do you suppose Aunt Vivien's turned into?"

Lewis repressed a shudder. "With any luck we'll never find out."

"So what about the Fount of All Knowledge?"

"My computer has changed, like most other things, but it still did roughly what I expected it to do. It gave me information."

"Really useful information, too," Greg said sarcastically.

"Well, that's the point," Lewis said. "It must be useful to me."

"But you don't understand it."

"I didn't," Lewis corrected him, "not until I worked out what was going on. The Fount of All Knowledge must mean somebody or something that I see as the source of all knowledge."

He gave Greg a few seconds to think about it, then said, "It's Mr Calvert."

"You mean the guy at the library you drone on about? 'Mr Calvert said this,' 'Mr Calvert said that.'"

"I didn't know you were listening," Lewis said coldly.

"I was trying not to, but some of it seeped through anyway. So the mirror meant that we should go and see Mr Calvert?"

Lewis nodded vigorously. "After all, he was the one that gave me the book in the first place."

"I suppose it kind of makes sense," Greg conceded, "as long as you don't think about it too hard."

"That should be easy enough for you, then," Lewis muttered under his breath.

"What?"

"I said, we'd better get over to the library... before things get any worse."

Greg nodded. "Let's just hope those Valkyries have gone back to Venezuela."

"Valhalla."

"Wherever."

They stepped outside, carefully closing the boathouse door after them.

"Listen," said Greg, "we'll just stroll over to the library, casually, like it was a normal day. That way we won't attract any attention."

He immediately set off in the wrong direction.

"It's this way," Lewis corrected him.

"I was going to take an indirect route, just in case."

"In case of what?"

"Are you going to give me a hard time the whole way? We wouldn't be in this fix if you hadn't brought that stupid book home in the first place."

Lewis took a deep breath to calm himself and followed Greg as he strode off towards the library, by the direct route.

They gave a wide berth to the many strange creatures they saw along the way. There was a blue-skinned hobgoblin in a park-keeper's uniform trying to catch a swarm of tiny, winged pixies in a butterfly net. He growled at the boys to keep off the flowers as he ran past. Elsewhere a small herd of unicorns was grazing on a patch of nettles where the tennis courts used to be.

Once outside the park they didn't see anyone they recognised, but there was no telling who these gremlins, trolls and leprechauns had been yesterday. There was a fairly steady stream of traffic on the road: individuals riding horses, oxen and lizards, as well as vehicles being pulled by all manner of beasts.

Greg appeared to have become inured to the strangeness. He even greeted the odd passer-by with a casual, "Hello there!" or "Nice day, isn't it?" Certainly everyone seemed friendly enough and they saw no sign of the Valkyries, or Lindsay either. Still, Lewis found it harder and harder to act as though this were just a normal day and he was glad they only had another couple of streets to go before reaching their destination.

The library was Lewis' constant refuge from whatever troubles he was undergoing at school or at home, and he hoped that even now, in the midst of this chaos, it might still provide an island of sanity. That hope crumbled when the library came into view.

It had been transformed into a great sandstone pyramid with statues of animal-headed deities posing on the ledges that ran all round the walls. A pair of sphinxes squatted on either side of the steps that now led up to a set of brass double doors.

The boys climbed the steps hesitantly and halted before the doors, looking for a handle, or even a bell pull. In the absence of either, Greg reached out to push the nearest door, but before his fingers touched the metal, they both swung open of their own accord.

As soon as they were inside, the doors slammed shut

behind them with a deep boom. The interior was as big as three football pitches. Rows and rows of shelves stretched away into the distance, each one crammed with piles of parchment scrolls. Mysterious hooded figures drifted here and there, removing scrolls then sitting at small desks before carefully unrolling them. The huge room was lit by oil lamps set in the walls and by flaming bowls set atop iron tripods.

The boys walked forward, their footsteps echoing on the polished marble floor. They came to a desk where a hook-billed bird on a perch clucked at the boys as they approached. The woman seated at the desk was busy making an entry in a large, leather-bound ledger with a quill pen, but the bird's agitated noise made her look up.

It was Miss Perkins, the assistant librarian, in the guise of an ancient priestess. Her narrow face was surrounded by an elaborate headdress and an ornate gold necklace hung around her thin neck. She raised her eyebrows challengingly at the two boys and scrutinised them disapprovingly.

Lewis only plucked up the nerve to speak to her after Greg had prodded him twice in the ribs.

"Miss Perkins, we need some help."

The assistant librarian's expression became even more suspicious. "Are you initiates?" she asked.

Lewis looked to his brother for help but was met with blank incomprehension. "Yes, we are," he answered, hoping that was the right thing to say.

"Then where is your token of wisdom?" Miss Perkins demanded in a pinched voice.

Lewis had no idea what she could be talking about. Seeing him at a loss, Greg interposed hurriedly. "He left it in his other trousers. You know how it is."

The excuse earned him a stony stare.

"Only an initiate may enter the Sanctum of Wisdom," Miss Perkins warned them darkly.

As if to add weight to her words, the bird ruffled its feathers and bobbed its beak threateningly.

Lewis had a sudden flash of inspiration. "No, I've got it here," he said, feeling around in his pocket. He pulled out his library card and presented it to Miss Perkins' dissatisfied gaze.

She examined it for a few seconds, then said grudgingly, "Very well, you may pass."

Before she could dismiss them, Lewis said, "Actually, we need to see Mr Calvert."

Miss Perkins looked shocked. "You use the high priest's name lightly. What business have you with him?"

Lewis tried to think of an adequate reply. Failing to come up with one, he opened his backpack and pulled out *The Folklore of Time.* "I have to return this book to him."

Miss Perkins wrinkled her nose up at the book as if he'd just presented her with a rat sandwich. She tilted her head to view it from a different angle. "This is no manner of sacred scroll known to me," she said haughtily.

"That's exactly why I have to take it to Mr Calvert," Lewis explained.

Miss Perkins winced, as though hearing the "high priest's" name used so openly was physically painful. She sniffed. "Third floor, room one."

She dipped her quill in the inkpot and returned to her notes. The bird made a gesture with its beak that left them in no doubt they were being dismissed.

"Over this way," Greg said too loudly, beckoning towards an arch beyond which a flight of stairs curled upwards. With one accord, all the hooded figures lurking among the shelves turned towards them and said, "Shhhh!"

The sound echoed through the vast hall like the crash of a tidal wave.

"You and your big mouth," Lewis muttered.

Greg made a face and walked through the arch.

They climbed the spiral stairway in silence and emerged in a long gallery lined with mummy cases. Greg walked over to the nearest one and stared it right in the eye. "Kind of looks like Wendy Armitage," he observed. "She's always slapping on too much make-up."

He started feeling down the side of the case for a way to open the lid. Lewis hurriedly pulled him away.

"Are you out of your head?" he said. "Don't we have enough trouble already?"

Greg looked at the case and thought about an old horror film he had seen on TV a few weeks ago. "Maybe you're right," he conceded.

Lewis pointed out the single door at the far end of the gallery. As they drew closer they could read the sign on it:

> *Seekers of knowledge only.*
> *All others report to the front desk.*

"You see, this must be the Fount Of All Knowledge," Lewis said with satisfaction.

"It took you long enough to figure it out," Greg told him. He walked up to the door and knocked twice. There was no answer. He reached for the doorknob.

"You can't just walk in," Lewis said.

"What do you want to do? Stand around here all day? It's going to be a *long* day, remember."

Lewis made a humphing noise. "Let me go first. He knows me."

Slowly he pushed open the door. The room beyond was surprisingly small after the great hall downstairs and the grand gallery that led here, but it was just as impressive in its own way. Fires burned in braziers along the walls, their light reflecting on the surface of a glass sphere that almost filled the room..

It was a huge crystal globe about five metres across, set upon a square base of black obsidian. Inside it clouds of sparkling mist swirled about restlessly.

"What do we do now?" Greg asked, once the door was securely closed behind them.

"Get closer, I suppose."

As they approached, the mists cleared to reveal a slight, stoop-shouldered figure sitting on an ornate wooden chair in the middle of the sphere. It was Mr Calvert, the head librarian. He was still recognisable, even though he had sprouted a long, white beard and wore a tall pointed hat on his bald head. He had a packet of digestive biscuits in his lap and was nibbling at them with his large, rabbit-like teeth. When he noticed the visitors, he guiltily set the biscuits aside and stood up, adjusting his rimless spectacles as he did so.

He peered through the glass, his brow furrowing as he strained to identify the boys.

"Ah, Lewis!" he said. Lewis was relieved to hear the welcome in his voice.

The head librarian hastily brushed some crumbs from the front of his robe and drew himself up with dignity.

"Do you come in search of knowledge?" he asked grandly.

"Yes, definitely," Lewis answered.

Mr Calvert tutted as if someone had just returned a book with one of the pages folded down. "No, no, no. You are supposed to say, 'I come to drink deep of your wisdom.'"

"Oh, right. I come to drink deep of your wisdom." When he saw that Mr Calvert hadn't reacted, he added, "Is there anything else?"

Mr Calvert started as though he had been shaken out of a reverie. "Oh, sorry. No, that's fine. My mind wandered for a moment. That's the trouble with being the Fount Of All Knowledge. You find your thoughts straying to matters that aren't strictly relevant to the present situation."

"That's going to be a big help," Greg commented under his breath.

Mr Calvert peered at him over the top of his spectacles as though he had only just noticed him. "This must be your brother Gregory. He is exactly as described."

"What does he mean 'as described'?" Greg demanded. "What have you been saying about me?"

"Never mind that now," said Lewis. "Mr Calvert, we have some important questions. It's about this book."

He displayed *The Folklore of Time*.

Mr Calvert glanced at it without recognition. "Has it been improperly filed?"

"No, it's nothing like that. There's this rhyme inside, the Lokiday rhyme. We recited it last night and today everything is different."

"Different from what?"

"Different from the way it's supposed to be. Some sort of magic spell has changed everything. You didn't used to be sitting inside a crystal ball like this."

Mr Calvert quirked an intrigued eyebrow. "Really? Where did I sit?"

"Behind a desk," Lewis replied. "Don't you remember?"

"As I told you," Mr Calvert said, spreading his hands before him, "I have an awful lot stored in my head. It might be in there somewhere."

"Well, you've changed," Lewis continued. "Miss Perkins has turned into some kind of priestess; the library's become a temple. Yesterday it was nothing like this."

Mr Calvert was nodding.

"You look like you believe it all," Greg told the librarian.

"Why should he lie?" Mr Calvert responded matter-of-factly.

Greg shrugged. "I just didn't think it would be that easy."

Mr Calvert settled himself back in his chair and steepled his fingers under his chin. "Now start from the beginning and tell me everything," he said.

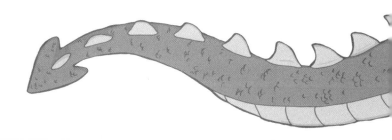

9. NO JOY IN THE KITCHEN

Lewis told the whole story of the book, the rhyme and everything they had been through that day, including the magic mirror and their flight from the Valkyries. He was just coming to his insight in the boathouse when he noticed that Mr Calvert had a faraway look in his eyes as though he weren't paying any attention.

"Mr Calvert!" he said loudly.

Mr Calvert looked at him owlishly. "Sorry. I was just recalling an amusing anecdote from Herodotus. Something to do with a hippo. Anyway, back to your problem. I suppose the first thing you need to know is why all this is happening."

"Yes," the brothers agreed at once. They both looked expectantly at Mr Calvert.

"Well, *I* don't know!" he exclaimed. "You have to work it out. You know what I've always told you, Lewis. Read first, then think, then conclude. Wisdom lies in the use of knowledge, not in its accumulation. Now, haven't you been researching matters of time for your school project?"

"You remember that?"

"You told me it a few minutes ago when you were explaining about the book. I'm not totally befuddled, you know. Now what have you learned about the days of the week and how they are named?"

"Well, Saturday is named after the Roman god Saturn, and Sunday and Monday are named after the sun and the moon."

"And the others?" Mr Calvert prompted.

"They're named after Norse gods. Let's see... Tyr, Odin, Thor and Freya."

"Yes, that's four." Mr Calvert nodded.

"The Vikings had five days," Greg interjected. "It's in the book."

"Five days," Lewis mused. "But we only use four of them."

"So what happened to the fifth day?" said Mr Calvert, raising his eyebrows.

"This is it!" exclaimed Lewis. "Lokiday. Loki's day."

"Who's Loki?" Greg asked.

"He was the Viking god of mischief, magic, that kind of stuff," Lewis explained.

"And does that fit in with what you've been seeing around you?" Mr Calvert asked.

Lewis pondered. "Yes, I suppose it does. But there's something else going on too."

"What exactly?"

"Time has stopped, Mr Calvert."

"So this day's going to last forever," Greg added.

"Hmm," Mr Calvert mused without any sign of concern. "It looks like I'll finally have time to catalogue those periodicals on the second floor."

The boys watched him cogitating, then Lewis finally said, "Mr Calvert!"

Mr Calvert looked up. "I hadn't drifted off that time," he informed them stiffly. "I was giving the matter a great deal of thought. A spell powerful enough to bring time to a halt must be potent indeed. If you knew anything about celestial mechanics you'd appreciate that. There is only one place where such a spell could have been found."

He paused dramatically.

"Are you going to share that with us?" Greg asked.

"Only *The Great Unholy Book* contains magic of such potency," Mr Calvert intoned darkly. He reached absentmindedly for a biscuit, as though seeking comfort in the face of such horror. "It is the unspoken tome, the monstrous grimoire, a book of dark horrors that strikes fear into the heart and blights the lives of the innocent."

He bit into the biscuit and chewed on it ferociously. As he did so a glazed look came over his eyes. Greg was about to say something but Lewis hushed him up. "He may be coming up with an important thought," he whispered.

Finally Mr Calvert came out of his daze and stared at them without recognition. Then he shook his head.

"Sorry, boys. What were we talking about? The wedding customs of the Chaldeans, wasn't it?"

"*The Great Unholy Book*, Mr Calvert," Lewis reminded him. "The monstrous grimoire."

"Ah yes. Only a spell from that book could stop time in its tracks. If you are to counter this pernicious magic, you must find the book and undo the spell."

"So where is the book?" Lewis asked.

Mr Calvert arched his eyebrows. "I haven't the least idea. But from what you say, it has been raised from its slumber by the Lokiday spell, right here in town."

"Well, then who's using it to stop time?"

"I'm afraid I can't help you there, either, Lewis, but maybe if you think about it..."

All at once Greg clutched his forehead and groaned.

"What is it?" Lewis asked. "Are you getting a headache?"

"Haven't you figured it out yet?" he asked. "You're the one who said we made a lot of this stuff the way it is. You know, Mum, Lindsay, Mr Calvert."

Lewis nodded and made his humming noise, unsure of just where this was going.

"So," Greg continued, "this horrible book that messes everything up..."

"Is Aunt Viven's cookbook!" Lewis finished for him, his jaw dropping at the revelation. "It has to be!"

He turned to Mr Calvert to look for confirmation. "Is that right?" he asked.

Mr Calvert was munching on another biscuit and staring upward. "Is what right?" he responded vaguely.

"Never mind him," said Greg. "We've found out what we need to know. Let's get out of here."

Lewis waved a farewell to Mr Calvert as they left, but the librarian was tapping a half-eaten biscuit against the end of his nose, completely lost in his own thoughts.

On the way down the stairs Lewis hurried to keep up with his brother who was taking them two at a time. "Where are we going?"

"Where do you think?" Greg retorted. "We're going home to get the book. We'll reverse the spell, start time up again, then hide out until the day's over."

"You make it sound so simple."

"One of us has to have a plan. If it wasn't for me, you'd still be up there yacking with that weirdo in the goldfish bowl."

They exited the library under the mistrustful eye of Miss Perkins and her unpleasant bird. As they crossed South Street, Greg rubbed his stomach.

"I don't know about you, but I could murder a mealie pudding."

"A good idea," Lewis agreed. "There must be some place around here where the food's edible."

They headed down Bridge Street to Moby Rick's fish and chip shop. It had changed quite a bit. For one thing, Rick was now a one-eyed pirate with a fruitbat perched on his shoulder. The food on offer consisted mostly of lizard, snake and blowfish, which the boys declined in favour of some innocuous looking cheese between slices of crusty bread.

It took all the coins they had in their pockets to pay for the snack, and Rick bit down on each one to make sure it was genuine. He threw in a flask of apple juice and invited the lads to join him on a planned pirate raid against Pittenweem. Refusing politely, the boys backed out of the shop and sat down on a wooden bench to eat.

Once the meal was over Greg stood up and

stretched himself. "Now I'm ready for anything!" he declared.

Lewis got up and brushed off the crumbs, wishing he shared his brother's confidence.

They approached the house cautiously, skulking at the corner until they were sure nobody was lying in wait for them.

"Do you think Aunt Vivien will be there?" Lewis asked.

"Could be," Greg said. "Best be prepared for the worst. Here's the plan. We walk in through the front door, we stroll into the kitchen and we get the book. Any questions?"

"That's it? You call that a plan?"

"What do you expect? Mission Impossible? It's our house. We live there. Just act normal and everything will be fine."

They walked casually up the street. Greg even put his hands in his pockets and started whistling. Lewis glanced around nervously, sure that the discordant noise would attract attention, but nobody came to their window.

They slowed down as a rickety wagon pulled by four frothing horses came careering up the street. It was manned by half a dozen goblins, each with a hand clamped on top of his head to stop his helmet falling off. A wolf was sitting up front with the driver, howling for all he was worth. In the back of the wagon were a couple of ladders and a huge wooden vat that was sloshing water in all directions as the vehicle veered from side to side across the road.

Lewis turned as it went by and saw that it was headed towards a plume of smoke somewhere in the region of the town hall.

"That was the fire brigade," Greg said in an amused voice.

"I'm surprised there aren't more fires," Lewis said. "You've seen what the school is like. It's only a matter of time before the whole town goes to pieces."

"We'll make sure it doesn't," Greg stated with iron determination.

Lewis didn't draw much strength from this. He could tell that Greg was just slipping into the role of a hero he'd seen in some film, and that this tough, in control attitude had nothing to do with any understanding of their situation or his ability to get them out of it.

They ignored the unholy howls of the Larkins' dog and the sound of it bashing against the fence as they walked up to their front door. The dinosaur that used to be Aunt Vivien's car was still sound asleep in the driveway.

Lewis put a hand on his brother's arm and said, "Maybe we should give this a bit more thought."

Greg answered with a smile of carefree self-assurance that made him feel even worse.

They entered the house, alert for whatever might be lurking inside. Walking up the hall, they could hear Mum tidying the bedrooms upstairs. She was singing her favourite Beatles' song "Yesterday" without any idea of how appropriate it was. The sound of her voice was so normal that it provided Lewis with a little comfort until he remembered that Mum was now seven feet tall and had a green tail.

They moved quietly through the front room and into the kitchen, where they were engulfed in a noxious cloud of greasy smoke. Overcoming the fumes, Greg pitched himself over the sink and flung open the window.

"What is Mum cooking?" Lewis choked, burying his nose in his sleeve.

There was a big fire set in an alcove in the wall roughly where the microwave used to sit. A huge, black pot hung over it and something bubbled frantically inside. They approached the pot as if it might explode and risked a look. The thick liquid inside was bright orange, and strange, multicoloured shapes floated in it.

"I'm glad we ate before we got here," Greg said weakly.

"The cookbook," Lewis said. "Where is it?"

They started searching the room. Although all of

the kitchen fixtures had been transformed into archaic equivalents, the layout was the same, and it didn't take them long to make the depressing discovery that Aunt Vivien's cookbook wasn't here.

"Do you have a plan B?" Lewis asked.

Greg picked up a rolling pin as big as his arm. "This is no time for jokes."

Before he could say another word the door banged open and Mum, all thirty stone of her, lurched into the room.

"Hello, boys," she greeted them cheerily. "Home for lunch?"

"No!" they chorused, their voices shaking.

Mum looked taken aback by their reluctance and not very pleased.

"We already ate," Greg explained.

"A lot," Lewis added, rubbing his belly and making an uncomfortable face for emphasis.

Mum dipped a spoon in the pot and took a sip. The boys could hardly bear to look.

"It's your loss," she told them reproachfully. "It's as fine a batch of salamander stew as I've ever made. It will probably last us for weeks."

Lewis fought to keep a pained expression from his face.

"It isn't one of Aunt Vivien's recipes, is it?"

"Good gracious, no! I wouldn't feed you any of those. I wouldn't want you to turn into scorpions or something."

"So what's happened to her cookbook?"

Mum looked puzzled. "You mean her spellbook?"

"That's what he means, Mum, the spellbook," said Greg. "He's just kidding." He forced a laugh and punched Lewis playfully on the arm.

Mum shrugged her brawny shoulders. "Vivien must have taken it with her."

"Taken it where, Mum?"

"She left with a gentleman friend," Mum said, raising her eyebrows meaningfully. "They were going for a drive down by the beach."

"Who was he?" Greg asked. He only just resisted adding, "And did he have a guide dog?"

"Mr Key I think he said his name was."

Lewis felt a shock shoot through him. "Lucas Oberon Key?"

"Oh, you know him," Mum said brightly. "That's nice."

"Do you know him?" asked Greg.

"He's the one that wrote the book, *The Folklore of Time*," Lewis said excitedly.

Greg looked confused. "What would he be doing here? And why would he take Aunt Vivien out on a date? Why would *anybody* take Aunt Vivien out on a date?"

"That carriage we saw outside this morning... that must have been his," Lewis said.

Greg made a disgusted face. "Why do I get the feeling this isn't good news?"

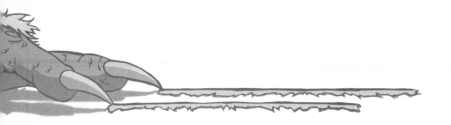

10. TIRED OF THE VALKYRIE

Mum dragged a wooden tub out from under one of the counters and stuffed the laundry into it. She then filled a bucket from a hand pump and tipped it into the tub. She was singing "Hey Jude".

"Mum, do you know where this Mr Key lives?" Lewis interrupted her.

Mum paused in her work and her brutish features took on a thoughtful expression that didn't look very at home there. "In the castle, down by the harbour."

"St Andrews Castle?" said Greg. "But that's a ruin."

"I don't think it's a ruin any more," said Lewis.

"Vivien was quite impressed," Mum said airily. "Pass me the soap, please, Greg."

Greg looked about and saw a wooden cup filled with white flakes. He handed these to Mum and she dumped them into the tub.

"What do you think?" he asked Lewis.

"It looks like we're going to the castle," Lewis answered.

"Why did she take the spellbook with her?" Greg complained.

"That was Mr Key's idea," Mum told them as she stirred the laundry with a long wooden spoon. "He insisted. To tell you the truth, I think he's some kind of sorcerer."

"Oh great!" Greg exclaimed.

"Perhaps he cast the spell that stopped time," Lewis said to Greg.

"What was that, son?" Mum asked.

"Time has stopped, Mum," Lewis explained. "This day is never going to end."

"Maybe I'll finally get through all my housework for a change then," Mum said breezily, turning her attention back to the washing.

"Come on, we'd better get a move on," Greg said, heading for the front door.

"Why don't you take a snack with you?" Mum chimed after them.

"Sorry, Mum, we'll pass on that!" Greg called back.

An idea suddenly dawned on Lewis. "Wait a minute! His initials: *L. O. Key*... He must be—"

Before he could complete the thought, Greg opened the door and they came face to face with a Valkyrie.

Greg immediately slammed the door in her face and clicked the lock in place. He said something he wouldn't have wanted Mum to overhear, even in her present condition.

"The back door!" they said together, and made a bolt for it.

But Mum had already come out of the kitchen to answer a pounding at the back door. She opened it to Shona Gilhooley, who brushed right past her.

At the sight of the two boys, the chief Valkyrie threw her head back and laughed. It seemed to be a habit. Two more Valkyries appeared behind her.

"Did you truly think we wouldn't be waiting for you?" she mocked.

"Frankly, we've been giving you as little thought as possible," Greg told her. "You're getting to be a real pain."

The Valkyrie leaned forward menacingly. "Are you going to surrender," she asked, "or are you going to offer me some sport first?"

Greg looked past her and deliberately widened his eyes in fake astonishment. "No, Mum, don't do it!" he screamed in a horrified voice.

All three Valkyries looked behind them. By the time it dawned on them that it was a trick, the boys were already halfway up the back stairway.

"I can't believe they fell for that!" said Lewis.

"Anybody who dresses the way they do can't be too bright," Greg said. "But we still have to get out of here."

"My room," Lewis said. "The magic mirror."

They tumbled into the room, slamming the door shut after them.

Greg stood in front of the mirror and said, "Mirror, mirror on the wall, are you any use at all?"

The Face blinked into view and raised an eyebrow. "That's hardly very tactful," it complained. "Besides, you should know the drill by now."

"Lindsay!" Lewis gasped.

"Hullo!" the mirror responded brightly.

"Valkyries chasing us," Lewis told it. "Have to escape."

"Use the rug," the Face suggested.

Greg looked down at the rug they were standing on. "Does it fly?" he asked hopefully.

"No, you simpleton. When they come in, you pull it out from under them. By the sound of things, you'd better get in position right now."

The boys moved to the far end of Aunt Vivien's ghastly rug and took a tight grip. The door burst open and Shona rushed in with one of her sisters.

"Now!" Greg cried.

They tugged with all their might, yanking the rug out from under the warrior women's feet. The Valkyries went down in a tangle of chainmail and swords.

Greg and Lewis jumped over them and bounded out into the hallway.

"Hey, babe," they heard the mirror say, "you are definitely the fairest of them all. And believe me, I should know."

An angry battle cry rang out, followed by the sound of glass shattering.

"He had that coming," Greg muttered.

At the top of the stair they saw more Valkyries heading up towards them. Greg immediately grabbed the hatstand and held it like a battering ram.

"Give me a hand!" he ordered Lewis.

Lewis took hold and as the first of the Valkyries reached the top step the brothers charged. They caught her full in the midriff with the end of the hatstand and sent her cannoning backwards into her sisters. All three tumbled back down the stairs while Greg pitched the hatstand aside.

"Follow me!" he urged, seating himself on the bannister. He shoved off and slid down at high speed.

Lewis jumped onto the bannister and followed. He'd always hated doing this; only Greg's dares had forced him into it before. He reached the bottom, came flying off, completely out of control, and fell right into Greg's arms.

Greg set him on his feet and they rushed out the front door.

The Chiz was waiting for them out on the pavement.

He looked only marginally less massive than the average mountain. He clamped an enormous hand on Greg's shoulder and said, "Back to school, Greg. Mrs Witherspoon wants you."

Greg wriggled ineffectually and began coughing. "Can't make it, Chiz," he wheezed. "I'm sick. Go ask my mum. I'm just on my way to the doctor."

He let loose another barking cough to emphasise the point.

"He's a wreck, Chiz," Lewis put in. "He should be in hospital."

"Big trouble if I don't bring you back," the Chiz said, slowly shaking his head. Lewis half expected some snow to fall off it.

"You'll be in bigger trouble if I die on the way there," Greg countered, working up another coughing spasm.

Thoughts were stirring in Chiz's head with the sluggishness of a tectonic shift, when they heard an all too familiar sound. It was the ululating battle cry of the Valkyries, who came pouring out of the house with vengeance in their eyes.

Greg wriggled as hard as he could and Lewis tried vainly to prise the Chiz's fingers loose. The Chiz seemed to hardly notice their efforts. He was gawking at the Valkyries as they formed a circle around the boys.

"This time there is no escape for you!" Shona Gilhooley declared, once she had finished laughing.

"Later, girls," Greg said dismissively. "We're with the yeti. Tell them, Chiz."

"He's going to school," the Chiz told the women flatly. He squeezed Greg's shoulder to show that he meant it.

"He is coming with us," Shona stated, grasping the hilt of her sword. Her friends all did likewise.

Lewis stepped close to the Chiz and said, "Chiz, we need to get out of here!"

"Sorry, Miss. We need him for target practice," Chiz apologised as he steered Greg towards the edge of the circle of warrior women.

Shona Gilhooley struck a martial pose and pointed her sword directly at Chiz's face.

"Not a step further, grotesque one!" she warned.

The Chiz looked puzzled for a second. Then he opened his wide mouth and bit the end off her sword. He chewed noisily before swallowing.

Shona stared in disbelief. Then her face turned crimson with fury.

"Get him!" she yelled.

The other five Valkyries obeyed without hesitation and piled on to the Chiz. Greg took his chance to squirm free and race off down the street, pulling Lewis along behind. He glanced back to see the Chiz tossing Valkyries this way and that, grinning inanely.

They had not gone far when they heard an ominous sound up ahead, like the roar of an engine mingled with the growl of a beast. All six of the roadsteeds came swerving round the corner and pulled up in front of them. Their eyes blazed like hot coals and gusts of steam blasted from their nostrils. They bucked up and down, their wheels whirling.

Both boys skidded to a halt.

"Think of a plan!" Greg said desperately.

"You mean one that doesn't end with them pounding us into the ground?" Lewis quavered.

"Yes, one of those."

The roadsteeds roared and they surged forward, speeding round and round the brothers in a tight circle.

"Have you thought of a plan yet?" Greg asked above the din.

Lewis shook his head. He was starting to feel dizzy.

A voice called out a command and the roadsteeds halted their frantic motion to make way for Shona and two of her sisters.

"Yvonne, Trisha, seize them!" Shona ordered.

The women quickly grabbed Greg and Lewis and trussed them up with thick lengths of rope.

The other three Valkyries were still locked in a

heroic struggle with the Chiz. It wasn't going their way. One had her arms wrapped uselessly around the Chiz's knee while the other two ducked under his huge fists, which swung back and forth like a pair of sledgehammers.

"Chiz, we could use a little help over here!" Greg shouted.

Shona cuffed him across the mouth. "Silence, fool!" she spat.

She picked him up and threw him across the front of her roadsteed. One of her sisters bundled Lewis up in the same fashion.

At a command from their leader, the other Valkyries abandoned their battle with the Chiz and ran for their steeds. All six Valkyries mounted up and roared off.

"I'm gonna be in trouble now, Greg!" The Chiz shouted after them.

"You think you've got problems!" Greg called back as the road sped by beneath him.

They raced down Largo Road and up Bridge Street.

Greg twisted his head to look up at his captor. "Are we going anywhere in particular or is this just a joy ride?" he asked over the roar of the roadsteed.

"You will see soon enough," she answered coldly.

As they swung past the West Sands and on to the Scores, Lewis saw a stampede of kelpies galloping along the beach. The bright green water horses shook their black manes and plunged headlong into the waves, kicking up a cloud of spray behind them.

The Valkyries coasted down to the castle, which, as Lewis had predicted, was no longer a ruin. Great stone walls reared up to where armoured figures patrolled the battlements and fiery banners fluttered from the lofty towers.

"I don't think we're going to like it here!" Greg shouted to his brother.

A heavy drawbridge crashed down over the moat and they raced across it to an arch that swallowed them up like the mouth of a colossal beast.

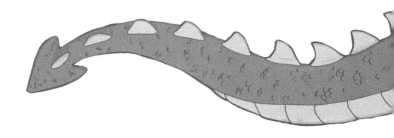

11. CONVERSATION WITH A CONMAN

The Valkyries halted their steeds in the middle of the courtyard. They dismounted and dragged Greg and Lewis on to their feet. The boys were untied, but two of the Valkyries gripped them tightly as their chief led the way into the keep. The doors opened before them, admitting them to a stone hall lit by flickering torches, which ended at the foot of a wide, granite stairway.

They stumbled up the steps and down a long passage decorated with carved images of dragons, snakes and club-wielding giants. A wooden door painted with flames swung open to reveal a spacious, well-lit chamber with a vaulted ceiling.

The walls were decorated with swords, spears and animal skins, except for the back wall, over which hung a russet curtain. The floor was covered in rugs patterned with red and orange flames. A man sat at a desk in the middle of the room. He rose from his chair and ambled towards them.

He wore a green suit and scarlet shirt with a black tie. A bright yellow handkerchief protruded from his breast pocket. His long hair was a blazing red, shot through with gold, and swept back from his lean, wily face. A small beard tapered out from his chin and his welcoming grin exposed two rows of sharp white teeth.

At a signal from the man in the green suit, the Valkyries released their captives and took up position by the door.

"Come on in, boys," the man greeted them. "Don't be shy. I've been waiting a long time to meet you. All day in fact."

As Greg and Lewis drew closer, he reached back to his desk and flipped open a box of cigars, selecting one.

"You're Lucas Oberon Key," said Lewis. "Or should I say, Loki, the god of mischief."

The man in green chuckled. "Guilty as charged." He tipped the cigar back and forth between his fingers. "I usually am."

Greg scowled. "So you're behind all this."

"Me?" Loki retorted, innocently laying a hand over his heart. "All I did was write the book. It was the two of you who unleashed the magic by saying the rhyme."

"So it only works if two people recite it," said Lewis.

Loki nodded. "It's one of the safety features of really

big magic. One idiot can't stir up this sort of mayhem by himself. He has to persuade another idiot to help him."

"You'd better watch who you're insulting, Loki," Greg bristled.

"Oh, I am grateful to you boys," said the god of mischief. "Never doubt that for a moment."

"Then why don't you let us go?" Lewis asked.

Loki gave him a sly look. "I never repay a favour. It would be bad for my image. After a couple of millennia out of the picture, that's something I have to work on."

"For a god, you don't look like much," Greg told him.

"I never was a god, in the strict sense of the word," Loki corrected him. "I was a fire giant by birth, not one of the Aesir, like Odin and the rest. I was sort of an adopted god, I suppose. And believe me, the rest of them gave me some stick about that! Why do you think I was so peeved all the time?"

"But you can do magic, can't you?" Lewis asked.

"My powers aren't what they were, but I still have a few tricks up my sleeve." A small flame sprouted from the end of Loki's finger and he used it to light his cigar. He drew in the smoke deeply, expelling it through his nostrils as a thin, sulfurous vapour.

"I bet you couldn't even light that cigar without a match if it wasn't your special day," Lewis surmised.

Loki exhaled a smoke ring and raised an eyebrow. "You're a pretty smart kid. Yes, as men became less dependent on us gods, it got to the point where we each had to settle for one day when we could come down and meddle in their affairs. On his day Odin would spread wisdom. Thor would make a lot of thunder, so that was a good day to stay indoors. Me, I'd sneak around playing little tricks and working mischief. It was hilarious. Then when I started pulling pranks on the other Aesir, they got mad and had my day yanked out of the calendar.

"Odin, in his supposed wisdom, exiled me, and I wandered the earth for centuries, immortal but powerless, waiting for my chance to make a comeback. During that time the Aesir must have dozed off, or their power just drained away, so you don't hear much out of them any more. Me, I managed to scrape a living gambling, conjuring, selling used cars, that kind of thing. But I still had a hankering for the good old days. That's why I wrote that book."

"*The Folklore of Time*," said Lewis. "It could do with an index."

"It was meant to be a mess, so it wouldn't attract too much attention," Loki explained, "so that nobody would realise its true purpose. The Lokiday rhyme was the only part that counted. I had to sneak it in somewhere

where none of the other gods would notice, just in case they were snooping around. Then all I needed was for somebody to come along who wanted the spell to be true so much that he could make it work. You know, somebody gormless enough to believe in that sort of balderdash."

"You need to watch your mouth, Loki," Greg scowled.

"Kid, I've insulted better and wiser men than you. That's part of my job description."

"So when did you get to town?" Lewis asked. "Were you here yesterday?"

Loki shook his head and took a puff on his cigar.

"When the spell started to take effect it sucked me right here, to the centre of things. It's kind of a shame, because at the time I was in Las Vegas sitting on a straight flush. To be honest, it's been so long since I wrote that book, I'd pretty much forgotten about it. I was hardly even aware of my true nature any more. But when I felt the magic pulling at me, it all came rushing back and I knew exactly what was happening."

"I don't get it," said Greg. "How does a cheap conman like you pull off something this big?"

Loki's mouth twitched irritably at the insult. "The way I figure it is this," he said: "every week on Lokiday, a little bit of magic used to leak into the world, just enough to cause a few laughs. Now, when there was no more Lokiday, there was no place for the magic to go, so for centuries it's been building up and building up, like water behind a dam."

"And now it's all burst out at once," said Lewis.

Loki leaned back against his desk and blew a plume of smoke at the vaulted ceiling. "Bingo, kid. Pretty spectacular, isn't it? For now it's just this little town of yours that's been transformed, but the magic is spreading even as we speak. Pretty soon it will be Lokiday all over the world."

"Only if we let you get away with it," Greg warned him.

Loki laughed. "And how are you going to stop me?"

Greg sputtered angrily. "We started this thing and we'll find a way to finish it. Won't we, Lewis?"

Lewis felt his stomach sink. Loki seemed so sure of himself; he didn't see how they could beat him. "I suppose maybe... maybe..." he stammered, "maybe we could... you know..."

Suddenly his eyes grew wide as he spotted a large book with a mottled cover on the desk behind Loki. Aunt Vivien's cookbook.

"I admit you boys sparked all this off," said Loki, "and whatever was going on in your heads at the time influenced how things turned out. What's more, you haven't been changed by the spell. I hadn't counted on that."

Greg noticed that Lewis was shuffling across the floor, trying to edge his way around Loki, and when his eyes lighted on the book, he understood why.

"Don't think we're finished yet," he asserted loudly, distracting the Viking god's attention. "This is our town and we're not letting you turn it into your own private play park. Like Shakespeare says, 'Tomorrow is another day.'"

"I think you're getting your quotes mixed up," Loki smirked. "Besides, tomorrow isn't coming, thanks to this."

He reached back and snatched up the book, just as Lewis made a grab for it. Loki flicked some ash from his cigar and it exploded in a plume of smoke right at Lewis' feet, sending him scurrying back to Greg's side.

"So it *was* you who used Aunt Vivien's book to stop time," Greg accused.

"All true," Loki said, casually flipping through the yellow pages. "My magic powers may be rusty, but I could smell this thing a mile away, wafting sorcery through the air like an old cheese gone bad. There's stuff in here even I'd be afraid to try."

"It's just irresponsible, tampering with time like this," Lewis objected. "You could be endangering the whole universe."

Loki waved his cigar around airily. "That's just part of the fun."

"But it's chaos out there," said Lewis. "What's going to become of everybody if this madness continues?"

"Serious-minded tyke, isn't he?" Loki commented, giving Greg a playful wink.

"Why don't you swallow that cigar and choke on it?" Greg growled.

Loki shook his head and tutted.

"You know, you boys don't really fit in. I'm going to have to do something about that. This is my day, and on my day everything goes the way I want it to. Call me a control freak if you like, but I'll have to make an adjustment where you're concerned."

"What about Aunt Vivien?" Lewis demanded. "What have you done with her?"

"I did have to string her along for a while," Loki admitted, "in order to get my hands on the book and find the right spell. If you think my book's badly organised, you should try finding your way around this." He waved the book of spells then tossed it down on the desk.

"Sooking up to Aunt Vivien is sinking pretty low," Greg told him, "even for a creep like you."

Loki shrugged. "You do what you have to do."

"Where is she now?" Lewis asked.

"Relax. Pretty soon you're going to be neighbours. You'll have adjoining cells. Is that cosy or what?"

He gestured to the Valkyries. "Girls, show our guests to their quarters."

The warrior women marched forward and seized the boys by their arms.

"This place has got great dungeons," Loki told them with relish. "I'm not saying you'll love them, but you'll have to admit they have the right air of hopelessness."

"How long do you plan on keeping us here?" Greg demanded.

"Not long," Loki answered. "I'm having a few storm giants over for dinner later. They've been out of the scene for a long time and I expect they'll be fairly peckish."

"You had to ask!" Lewis moaned.

"You'd better watch out," Greg threatened. "There isn't a prison made that can hold us."

Loki dismissed them with a contemptuous wave and the Valkyries dragged them away.

"What did you say that for?" Lewis asked.

"Why not?" Greg retorted. "We may as well go out with style."

They were manhandled along a twisting maze of passages and stairways to a spiral of stone steps leading deep beneath the castle. Even the torches illuminating this underground prison seemed shrunken and wan, as if they, too, were infected with the dreariness of the place.

Shona pulled open the thick wooden door of the nearest cell and the two boys were pitched headlong inside. They landed flat on their faces in a heap of dirty straw.

"Relax!" Greg whispered. "Did you see that rusty old lock? With my Swiss army knife I can pick my way through it in seconds."

Before Lewis could respond, they were dragged roughly to their feet and manacled to the wall. When Greg yanked at his chains, he discovered they were securely fastened.

Shona treated them to a look of utter contempt. "Even this pigsty is too good for the likes of you," she sneered.

She slammed the door shut and they heard a key being turned in the lock.

"Thanks for the thought!" Greg shouted after her.

Lewis looked around the grimy, dank cell. The only light came through a small grille in the ceiling that admitted a faint trickle of torchlight from somewhere above. He thought he could see something rat-like twitching its snout in a far corner. He was glad the place wasn't well enough lit to reveal its full horror.

He turned to Greg. "What now, Houdini?"

"We have to get out of here," Greg said, oblivious to the sarcasm. "We need to get these chains off, open the door – and believe me, that part will be easy – grab the book and break out of this dump before Loki can catch us."

His brow furrowed in concentration. "Once we're through the door, there may be a guard outside. In that case, you go for his legs and trip him up and I'll take care of the rest. I'll put on his uniform and we can pretend you're a prisoner I'm escorting to another part of the castle. We already know the way to Loki's office. We hide outside and when he leaves, we sneak in and snatch the book. After that, we get down to the courtyard and grab a couple of those roadsteeds. Then we're gone."

"Should we concentrate on the first part for now?" Lewis suggested, rattling his chains.

"That's one of your biggest problems," Greg told him. "You never plan ahead. Everything is short term with you."

Lewis was resigning himself to a lecture, when the situation suddenly took a brighter turn. "I think I know how we can get loose," he announced.

"How?" Greg asked, following his brother's gaze. He groaned out loud.

Lindsay was hovering a metre off the floor with something that looked like a big star-shaped lollipop in her hand.

"Do we really want to be rescued this badly?" Greg asked out of the side of his mouth.

12. A RELUCTANT RESCUE

"Greg, have you noticed how much trouble you get into when I'm not around?" Lindsay asked as she floated towards them. "Doesn't that tell you something?"

Greg grimaced. Before he could say anything that might drive Lindsay away, Lewis interrupted. "What's that you've got, Lindsay?" he asked. At second glance, it was a slender shaft of wood topped by a crystal-blue star.

Lindsay turned her wide, bespectacled eyes upon him as though she were surprised to see him there.

"It's a magic wand," she replied, "and believe me, I had to call in a few favours to get it."

"So what does it do?" Greg asked sullenly. "Will it make us fly?"

"Oh, Greg, don't be so silly," Lindsay chided, batting her eyelashes. "What use would that be when you're all chained up? No, it's a wand of unlocking."

"Unlocking?" Greg repeated with grudging interest.

Lindsay nodded vigorously. "Yes, and you wouldn't believe how hard it was to come by," she confided. "I had to ask around a lot of fairies down at the magic ring, and Brenda McCracken made this big deal about what did I want it for, and who was I taking it to. So I told her that at least nobody had ever seen me dancing with the leprechauns on midsummer's eve..."

"Unlocking, eh?" Greg said again. "How does it work?"

"Oh, that part's easy." Lindsay smiled.

She gently tapped each of Greg's manacles with the wand. They instantly popped open and fell from his wrists.

"Nice trick," Greg said, stepping away from the wall.

"It's fully charged and can unlock just about anything," Lindsay enthused.

"That sounds like a handy thing to have," Lewis voiced loudly.

"You'd better set him free," Greg suggested, "before he gets cranky."

Lindsay flitted over to Lewis and tapped his manacles with the end of the wand. The chains fell away and Lewis rubbed his wrists. "How did you know we were here?" he asked.

Lindsay made a face. "Sally Kettles saw you being carried off by the Valkyries when she was gossiping with some selkies down by the burn. Of course, she couldn't wait to hurry back and start telling everybody that *Lindsay's boyfriend* was out riding with some blonde."

"What do you mean *Lindsay's boyfriend?*" Greg objected.

"You know how fairies like to tease," Lindsay explained with a toss of her head. "Of course, some of them *can* see into the future," she added wistfully.

"Maybe we should focus on getting out of here," Lewis snapped, quickly changing the subject.

Greg nodded and reached into his pocket for his Swiss army knife. Before he could decide which attachment to use as a lock pick, Lindsay floated over to the door and tapped the lock with her wand.

"You didn't need to do that," he told her peevishly as the door swung open. "I was all set to take care of it myself."

Shoving the knife back into his pocket, he snatched the wand from Lindsay's hand. "You'd better let me take care of this."

Lindsay pouted and spun about in the air.

"Lindsay!" Lewis said, before she could disappear. "Greg's just worried that this could be dangerous, so he needs to go first."

"All right," Lindsay conceded. "But there was no need to be so rude."

Lewis gave Greg a prod.

"Sorry, erm, Lindsay," Greg said, choking on the words. "I'm a little tense."

Lindsay flashed him a forgiving smile. "Just be careful with the wand, Greg," she cautioned.

Greg motioned the others to stay back while he poked his head out into the passage. "No sign of any guards," he reported.

"You just can't get good help," Lindsay commented. "Trolls are so unreliable."

Together they stepped outside and Greg started for the stairs.

"Greg!" Lewis said.

Greg looked back. "Now what?"

"What about Aunt Vivien?"

"What *about* Aunt Vivien?"

"We have to rescue her," Lewis reminded him. "Loki said she was in the cell next door."

Greg came back and warily eyed the door of the adjacent cell. "Do we have to?"

"You heard what Loki said. Even he couldn't figure out the book without her help."

"All right," Greg admitted. "But can you even imagine what kind of a monster she's going to be? Mum is an ogre and that's bad enough. Is there anything horrible enough for Aunt Vivien to be?"

"I admit it's a risk," Lewis admitted. "But whatever she's turned into, don't say anything to offend her. We need her help."

Greg edged closer to the door of the cell and grasped the wand tightly between sweaty fingers. "How does this thing work?" he muttered.

"You just give the lock a light tap," Lindsay told him, gesturing with her hand to show him how.

"I knew that," Greg snapped. "I don't need an instruction manual."

Lindsay let out an affronted "Ooh!" and disappeared in a shimmer of light.

Greg raised the wand and licked his lips, then froze as though his muscles were rebelling. "This is our last chance to walk away," he warned Lewis.

Lewis glared at him. He shrugged. "Okay, okay. But remember, it's Aunt Vivien in there. Expect mind-numbing horror."

Greg gave the lock a hesitant tap and the door swung open with an ominous creak of its rusting hinges. They peered into the cell and saw... the very last thing they expected.

Aunt Vivien was exactly the same.

The ornately styled, dyed hair, the overly made-up face, the frighteningly floral dress: none of it showed any sign of having been affected by the Lokiday rhyme. The only difference was that instead of wreaking havoc in their kitchen, she was manacled to the wall in Loki's dungeon.

"Well, it's about time somebody got here!" Aunt Vivien declared haughtily.

Neither Greg nor Lewis had been able to move beyond the open doorway.

"I don't understand," Greg murmured. "Why is she still the same?"

"Think about it for a moment," said Lewis. "Is there any way she could be scarier than she is normally?"

Greg shook his head.

"Are you two going to stand there all day?" Aunt Vivien asked shrilly. "You can't just leave me here like this."

"We could, you know," Greg muttered between clenched teeth.

"Come on, you'd better set her free," Lewis said. "Just think how much it will annoy Loki."

"You're right," Greg agreed with relish. "That is a silver lining."

He strode decisively across the cell and tapped Aunt Vivien's manacles with the wand. They fell away and Aunt Vivien stepped forward, straightening her dress as she did so.

"I assume Lucas has thought the better of his little prank and sent you to release me," she said tartly.

"Not exactly," Lewis said. "We were his prisoners as well."

Aunt Vivien tilted her head back and touched a hand tragically to her brow. "I knew it! He was only after one thing. My book. That Beast!"

"I'm afraid that's true," Lewis said.

"Why did you go along with him in the first place?" Greg asked disgustedly. "He's a total creep. Even you... I mean... you're not exactly... but..."

His voice faded away before Aunt Vivien's withering stare.

"He was very charming at first," she said coldly, "but then men are like that, aren't they?"

"If you say so," Greg mumbled.

Lindsay popped into existence in their midst and beamed at Aunt Vivien, who did not return the smile.

"A fairy," Aunt Vivien said disapprovingly. "I never thought that Adele's boys would take up with fairies."

"She's just a friend," Greg stated with emphasis.

"A very good friend," Lewis added quickly. "Without her we'd all still be in chains."

Aunt Vivien sniffed. "That's highly commendable, I'm sure. But I warn you, young lady: I don't hold with flitting about aimlessly from place to place, changing the colour of people's flowers. And isn't that dress a little skimpy for this time of year?"

"If you read *Pixipolitan* magazine, you'd know this is the latest fashion," Lindsay retorted.

"We don't have time for this right now," Lewis interrupted urgently. "We have to get the book back."

"Indeed we do!" Aunt Vivien affirmed. "Who knows what damage that cad might cause with it?"

"He's already causing damage," Lewis told her. "He's brought time to a standstill."

Aunt Vivien looked puzzled. "Why should he want to do that?"

"Maybe he likes daytime TV," Greg grunted.

Lewis gave him a warning look. "Aunt Vivien, do you know what day it is?" he asked.

"What a silly question," Aunt Vivien chided. "It's Lokiday, of course."

"Of course. What day was it yesterday?"

"What do you mean *yesterday?*" Aunt Vivien stared at him as though he were an idiot.

"The day before today," Lewis pressed her. "Don't you remember Thursday?"

Aunt Vivien shook her head. "Really, I don't know what's wrong with you young people today. How do you get these silly notions into your heads?"

Greg leaned close to Lewis' ear and muttered, "She looks the same, but her head is messed up just like everyone else's."

Turning to Aunt Vivien, he said, "Come on, let's get your book back from Loki."

Aunt Vivien humphed. "When I see him I shall give That Beast a good piece of my mind, you mark my words. There was a boy from Tillicoultry I once had to give a good talking to…"

"Let's get going," Greg interrupted.

"Right," Lewis agreed. "We need to stay really quiet." He looked at his three companions and shook his head. "At least as quiet as we can manage."

Greg stuck the magic wand into his belt and stepped out of the cell. He led the little party up the stairway to a stout wooden door with a metal grille set into it at head height. Greg turned to the others and touched a finger to his lips.

A loud rumbling sound was coming from the passage beyond. When he pressed his face to the grille, Greg could see out of the corner of his eye a troll seated upon a stool that looked far too flimsy to support him. The troll wore a metal breastplate and helmet and was leaning back against the wall with his eyes shut. The noise they could hear was his snoring.

A tap of the wand unlocked the door and they all moved carefully out into the passage. All except Lindsay. She blinked out of sight and materialised directly over their heads as they tiptoed past the troll. Startled by her sudden appearance, Greg jumped back and collided with Lewis, who collided in turn with Aunt Vivien.

Aunt Vivien gave a yelp and grabbed something to stop herself falling over – the troll's bulbous nose.

As soon as she saw what she'd done she yanked her hand away, but it was too late. The troll cracked open two piggy eyes and heaved himself to his feet, snatching up a huge club that was propped against the wall at his side.

Everyone froze on the spot.

The troll stood as still as any of them, his brow furrowed as he pondered what he was supposed to do in a situation like this. Eventually he worked it out and bellowed, "Halt!" with enough force to loosen a few flakes of plaster from the ceiling.

Greg, Lewis and Lindsay all recoiled. Lewis wondered if the four of them could bring the creature down without getting their skulls split open.

Aunt Vivien stepped squarely in the troll's way and wagged a finger at him.

"I don't think Lucas will be very pleased to learn that his guards take their duty so lightly!" she shrilled right in the troll's face. "I hardly call sitting there snoring an example of military discipline!"

The troll opened his mouth to speak but Aunt Vivien silenced him with a poke in the chest.

"You call yourself a guard? Suppose there had been some really dangerous prisoners locked in the dungeon? They'd be loose in the castle now, causing all manner of mayhem, and whose fault would it be? Yours, young man, and nobody else's!"

The troll backed off, his face a contorted mask of fear, but Aunt Vivien pursued him mercilessly. Greg and Lewis could feel her shrewish voice grating so painfully at their own ears, they almost felt sorry for the dull creature.

The troll felt behind him for the wall, but found only emptiness. Too late he realised he had backed onto the open stairway. With a snort of alarm he dropped his club and went tumbling backwards. His helmet clanged off the stone steps as he bounced nose over tail all the way down to the dungeons.

"I don't know what Lucas expects, employing such riff-raff," Aunt Vivien sniffed. She picked up the fallen club and a steely look came into her eye. "Let's pay a call on him and see what he has to say for himself."

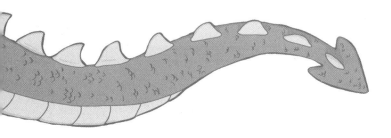

13. PLAYING WITH FIRE

Greg took the lead with a bold stride that was intended to give the impression he knew what he was doing.

"Are you sure you know the way?" Lewis asked.

"Relax. I've got it all mapped out in my head," said Greg, tapping his temple, "just like Lawrence of Antarctica."

"Arabia," said Lewis, but Greg wasn't listening.

As they negotiated the maze of passages, Greg's footsteps began to falter until he came to a stop by a wooden door.

"I think we came from that way," Lewis said, tilting his head towards the far end of the passage.

"Think? Think's not good enough. You have to know, and I know we came this way."

Greg opened the door and stepped into the castle kitchen.

None of the servants, human and other, who were scurrying about inside, paid him any attention. Huge iron pots were bubbling furiously and giving off aromatic clouds of steam. Broad, silver platters were piled high with exotic fruits and generous cuts of meat.

Greg inhaled the mixture of culinary smells and asked, "When did we last eat?"

"I don't know," Lewis replied, displaying his useless digital watch. "No time, remember?"

"Well, it feels like ages."

Greg reached for a slice of cured ham and caught the attention of a wiry, fur-covered creature in a lofty chef's hat, who immediately cried out, "*Zut alors!*"

Lewis grabbed Greg's arm and dragged him back out into the passage, slamming the door shut after him. He pointed to Aunt Vivien, who was marching off the other way.

Greg stifled a cry of alarm and ran to overtake her. There was no telling what trouble she might stir up if she wandered off by herself.

"You'd better let us go in front," he cautioned as he elbowed past her, "just in case."

"In case of what?" she demanded.

"In case of *anything*," Greg insisted, blocking her attempt to get past him.

Lewis caught up with him and whispered, "That was close."

"You need to keep a better eye on her," Greg told him.

"Why me?"

"Because my eyes can't take it," Greg whispered.

"I think it's this way," Lindsay advised them from above. She pointed to an open archway.

"That's just what I was going to say," Greg declared.

Once through the arch, they were immediately brought up short by the sound of marching feet coming the opposite way. Everyone looked wildly around until Lewis said, "Here!"

He had lifted the edge of a hanging that showed a dragon biting the head off a knight. Behind it was an alcove with just enough space to accommodate all four of them. They squeezed in side by side, the rough weave of the hanging brushing against the ends of their noses.

Accompanying the clomp of many heavy feet, came a score of loud voices raised in raucous song. The words were in a guttural tongue they did not recognise, but the tune was uncannily close to "Walking in a Winter Wonderland".

Once the noise had safely passed them by, they emerged from their hiding place.

"What were those things?" Greg wondered, looking towards the far end of the passage from where their crude singing could still be faintly heard.

"More trolls," Aunt Vivien answered, wrinkling her

nose with displeasure. "I'm surprised even a reprobate like Lucas lets them sing that dreadful song in the confines of his castle."

"What's so dreadful about it?" Lewis asked.

Aunt Vivien raised her eyebrows. "If you were any sort of gentleman," she told him severely, "you wouldn't even ask."

"Let's concentrate on business," Greg said. He headed up the corridor where another stairway brought them to Loki's office.

Greg pressed his ear to the door then turned to the others. "I can't hear anything. I don't think there's anybody inside."

"That door's so thick they could be holding a football match in there and you couldn't hear it," Lewis pointed out.

"So what do you want to do?" Greg demanded impatiently. "Hang around until we're invited inside?"

"I'm just saying we need to be careful. Lindsay, you'd better stay here with Aunt Vivien."

"Stay here?" Aunt Vivien objected. "You forget that I have a score to settle with That Beast." She lifted the club and shook it.

"He may not even be in there," Lewis said, trying to calm her. "The important thing is to find the book and get away. You two wait here and we'll go in first."

"He may be more trouble than you can handle," Aunt Vivien warned.

"If we need help we'll whistle," Greg assured her dismissively.

He took hold of the large brass doorknob and opened the door just enough to ease himself sideways into the room. Lewis slipped in after him. There were the animal skins, the swords, the big desk, but no sign of Loki or anyone else.

They let out a joint sigh of relief and walked quickly across the fire-patterned rugs. The book was no longer on top of the desk. They lifted up the papers and ornaments that littered it, and examined the sides of the desk.

"There's a drawer here, but it's locked," Lewis said.

"Don't worry," Greg assured him, pulling the magic wand out of his belt. "I'm the man with the means."

"Thanks to Lindsay," Lewis reminded him.

"Fine. After this is all over we'll buy her some cupcakes"

He gave the drawer a tap and yanked it open. Sure enough, the book was inside and he pulled it out with a flourish. He stuck the wand in his belt and flipped through the pages.

"Most of this isn't even in English," he said disgustedly.

Lewis leaned over for a look and pursed his lips.

There were uneven lines of runic shapes, some stuff that looked like Greek, lots of star-shaped diagrams and drawings of toads, goats and other creatures inscribed in the margins.

"We'll just have to figure it out when we get home," he said, sliding the drawer shut.

"Sorry to throw a spanner in the works, boys, but you aren't going anywhere," said a voice, seemingly from nowhere.

Greg and Lewis spun around to see the russet curtain at the far end of the room sweep aside of its own accord. Beyond it Loki was rising from a divan on which he had evidently been taking a nap. He stretched his arms and walked towards them.

"You boys keep coming back on me like a bad hamburger," he said, lighting a cigar.

"We're going to give you more to worry about than indigestion," Greg threatened, brandishing the book.

"Why don't you put that thing down," Loki advised, taking a casual puff on his cigar. "You can't even read it. I admit that's a handy gadget you've got stuck in your belt, though. Too bad it won't save your hides."

He placed himself directly between the brothers and the door.

"Come on," Greg told Lewis. "We can take him."

He took an aggressive step towards the Norse god.

Lewis gulped and followed. He was sure this was a bad move, but their options were limited.

Loki grinned broadly and extended his empty hand, cupping it as he did so. "I'll tell you what I'm going to do. I'm going to give you a lesson in humility and I won't even charge you a penny for it."

He tipped the ash from the end of his cigar into the palm of his open hand. It immediately blazed into a roaring fireball that grew larger and larger without causing Loki any harm at all.

"Looks like the end of the line for you two," he said. "But before you go, I just want to thank you again for making my day."

Chortling at his own joke, he raised his hand, preparing to hurl the expanding fireball at the boys.

Greg lifted the book before him and stepped in front of Lewis.

"If you blast us, you'll lose the book too," he warned.

Loki smiled condescendingly. "You're missing the point, son. I don't need the book any more. The longer the day goes on, the more powerful I get, and remember, Lokiday will never end."

"Don't be too sure of that," said Lewis. "If you destroy the book, then all the magic you've made with it will be cancelled out."

"Really?" Loki responded quizzically. He quirked an

eyebrow and gazed thoughtfully at the ceiling for a few seconds. "No, I don't think so," he concluded. "I think it'll just stop the two of you from giving me any more headaches."

"Your headache is just about to start," Greg retorted, looking past the Norse god's shoulder. "This book is overdue and you're about to pay a big fine."

"Don't try to trick a trickster, son," Loki told him with a pitying shake of the head. "I was pulling the 'something's creeping up behind you' routine on Thor while you people were still painting bison on cave walls."

Loki's lip curled into a sneer. He raised his hand and the fireball blazed bright, expanding without even singing his sleeve.

While Loki's attention was directed towards the boys, Aunt Vivien had slipped into the room behind his back, and was poised to inflict her terrible vengeance upon him. Too late Loki saw in Lewis and Greg's eyes that this was no trick.

Before he could turn, Aunt Vivien hefted the troll's club and brought it down on his head with a sound like two empty oil cans banging together. Loki's face went slack. He did a complete pirouette and sank into a senseless heap on the floor.

"Good grief, have you killed him?" Lewis exclaimed.

"I shouldn't think so," Aunt Vivien said regretfully.

"He is a god after all, and they're a lot harder to kill than you or me."

Even as she spoke, Loki began to stir. He groaned and moved a hand sluggishly towards his head. Aunt Vivien took another swing and knocked him flat again.

"Beast!" she hissed at him.

"Let's get out of here!" Greg ordered, sticking the book under his arm.

Aunt Vivien dropped the club and snatched the book away from him. "It is mine after all," she pointed out peevishly.

"Let's just go before Loki wakes up and barbecues us," Greg snapped.

They dashed out past Lindsay who was floating by the door with an anxious expression on her face.

"Greg, you could have been hurt!" she gasped.

Greg paid no attention and they hurried down the stairway with Lindsay swooping behind.

"Do you have a plan for getting out of the castle?" Lewis asked as they reached the bottom of the steps.

"Sure," Greg answered bullishly. "It just needs some fine tuning."

"Like, how to get past the guards and over the drawbridge?" Lewis suggested.

"Those are the right questions," Greg answered, "and that's half the battle. I've told you that before."

They reached the front door of the keep and opened it a crack. Peering out at the courtyard, Lewis saw groups of trolls milling here and there. Some of them were playing crude games with rocks and bones, while others were matching strength in arm-wrestling or head-butting. Two of the brutish creatures were guarding the gate, each of them armed with an enormous battleaxe.

"Lucas keeps his carriage over there in the stables," Aunt Vivien said, pointing to the left.

"You mean the one with the giant goats?" Lewis asked.

"Yes, the giant goats," Aunt Vivien agreed. "Nasty, ill-smelling creatures, but he seems to like them. Birds of a feather, I say. He keeps them ready to leave at all times. He hates having to wait for anything."

"You know an awful lot about this guy considering you only met him this morning," said Greg.

"He's very talkative," Aunt Vivien said defensively.

Greg shrugged. "Right, we can handle the goats, but what about the drawbridge?" He tapped the magic wand. "Will this do the trick?"

Lindsay shook her head, making the light sparkle on her gem-encrusted spectacles. "It doesn't work on fortifications."

Greg chewed his lip meditatively. "I've got a plan," he said, "and it all depends on you, Lindsay."

Lindsay quivered excitedly and by the time he had explained his plan she was positively glowing. "That's very clever, Greg," she said admiringly.

Greg took a step back as she moved closer to him.

Lewis shook his head. He'd been caught up in Greg's schemes often enough to set alarm bells ringing. On the other hand, he reflected, maybe this wasn't the time for reason or caution. Greg had been devising crazy schemes for as long as they'd both been alive, and in the normal world, where the rules of logic and common sense applied, they never came to anything. But maybe here, in a world where lunacy was the norm, he was finally in his element.

"All right, let's go with that plan," Lewis said. "We still need to get to the stables without anybody noticing us."

"Trolls aren't too bright," Lindsay said hopefully.

Aunt Vivien had opened a nearby closet and was hauling out a pile of green cloaks. "These should do the trick," she announced.

"What is this stuff doing there?" Greg asked.

"It's where they put the dirty laundry," Aunt Vivien answered with a sniff. "Sometimes it's left there for weeks."

Lewis picked up a cloak and examined it at arm's length. It was heavily stained with mud and food, and it smelled badly of troll.

"We have to wear these?" Greg asked with distaste.

"I don't see any other way," Lewis said regretfully.

"I'll meet you at the stables," Lindsay said, and twinkled out of sight.

Aunt Vivien drew Lewis aside. "Don't get involved with a fairy," she counselled him. "They can't be depended on. You mark my words. There was one, a flower fairy called Violet Ray, and I heard that she—"

"Thanks for the advice, Aunt Vivien," Lewis cut her off, "but we have bigger problems right now."

"All right, but don't you forget – *fairies!*" She wagged a finger.

They pulled their cloaks around their shoulders, grimacing at the stench.

"If nobody looks too closely, the smell will let us pass for trolls," said Greg.

The three of them huddled together and set off across the courtyard. No one appeared to notice them until they were almost at the stables, where a passing troll grunted a greeting at them.

Greg grunted back as loudly as he could and this seemed to be sufficient to send the troll happily on his way.

"They are so uncouth," Aunt Vivien told Lewis. "Now when I was a girl, servants took pride in their appearance. We had a maid who used to launder her uniform every day. Every day. And her pinny was always freshly starched."

"Shh!" Lewis whispered desperately. "The trolls will hear you."

"Let them!" Aunt Vivien huffed. "It's about time somebody put them in their place."

"Later," Lewis advised.

They ducked into the stables and paused to adjust to the dimmer light. Lindsay was hovering in the air, glancing nervously at the Valkyries' roadsteeds rumbling and snorting in their stalls. The carriage sat in the centre of the floor, where the goats munched on a heap of dirty straw. The stink they gave off was enough to banish the smell of troll for a lifetime.

Lewis opened the door directly in front of the goats and light poured in. The goats continued to chew. Greg and Lewis bundled Aunt Vivien into the carriage then climbed up on the driver's seat, where Greg grabbed the reins.

"It's up to you now, Lindsay," Lewis said.

"Here I go," Lindsay beamed. "Wish me luck, Greg."

"Good luck," Greg mumbled. "She'd better not mess this up," he added as soon as she had skipped out into the courtyard.

Lindsay scampered up to the nearest group of trolls, who were playing a game of dice. She plucked the dice out from under their noses and ran off. With a furious bellow the trolls lumbered in pursuit, shaking their fists.

The next group of trolls was dipping their tankards into a barrel of ale and enjoying a round of coarse jokes. Lindsay plunged one hand into the barrel and splashed ale in their faces.

At first one of them laughed, thinking one of his fellows had done it. Then they saw the fleeing fairy and joined the angry pursuit. Whenever the mob got too close, Lindsay flitted into the air or winked out of sight to re-materialise behind them.

The trolls were in a frenzy of rage, and now Lindsay was racing directly towards the drawbridge. As she closed in, the whole mob of trolls made a lunge for her, hairy arms outstretched.

At the last possible instant she twinkled out of sight. The trolls hit the drawbridge like a twenty-car pile-up. The wood shuddered under the impact, and the ropes holding it upright snapped. Down crashed the drawbridge, and the trolls, yelling and cursing, poured over it in search of their quarry.

From inside the stables Lewis saw that Lindsay had carried out her part of the plan. "Come on!" he urged. "Let's go!"

Greg whipped the reins and shouted, "Off you go, lads!"

The goats went on chewing their straw.

Greg shook the reins as hard as he could. "Come on, mush! On Prancer! On Dancer! On Donner and Blitzen!"

The increasing panic in his voice had no effect. The goats were determined to remain exactly where they were and chew down every last shred of straw.

Lewis' heart sank. "If we don't get out of here fast, we're doomed!" he exclaimed.

14. THE NOT SO GREAT ESCAPE

At that moment Aunt Vivien leaned out of the carriage. "Move, you shiftless brutes!" she shrieked in a voice so shrill it hurt the boys' ears.

Straw dropped from the goats' jaws and they shot forward as if somebody had just stabbed them in the backside with red-hot needles. The sudden jolt almost threw Greg and Lewis from their seats, and before they could take in what was happening, they were careering across the courtyard at terrifying speed.

Loki leaned out of a high window and stabbed a furious finger at them. "Stop them, you peabrains!" he yelled, his face crimson with rage.

Most of the trolls were already across the drawbridge when his voice pulled them up short. When they turned they saw two gigantic goats charging straight at them, their heads lowered to batter their way through any obstacle in their path. The trolls by the gate had just enough wit to leap aside. Those on the drawbridge toppled into the water like skittles as the carriage thundered through their midst.

Lewis clung desperately to his seat as they rushed headlong down the road into town. "Can't you slow them down?" he gasped.

"It's all I can do not to fall off!" Greg panted, heaving vainly on the reins with all his strength.

They hit a pothole that bounced the carriage into the air like a sack of potatoes. It crash-landed with a bang and rumbled on.

"At least at this rate," Greg puffed, "I don't think anybody's going to catch us."

Lindsay materialised in front of them, but before she could even open her mouth, they rocketed past so fast that the rush of air sent her spinning. She tried to fly after them, but could not keep up, so she twinkled into the carriage onto the seat beside Aunt Vivien.

They swerved dizzyingly from street to street, with terrified pedestrians leaping for cover on all sides. Bouncing about like a ping-pong ball, Lewis could feel his bones rattling.

"Try to steer them towards home!" he urged Greg over the thunder of hooves.

"What do you think I've been trying to do?" Greg yelled back. He untangled his hands from the reins and flung them at his brother. "Here, you steer them!"

The goats swung sharply round a corner and the boys let out a cry of terror, clinging on for dear life. Inside the carriage Aunt Vivien was buffeted this way and that, almost crushing Lindsay beneath her.

"Stop this at once, you reckless animals!" she cried at the top of her lungs.

They burst into Market Street where some sort of fair was going on. A wave of terror passed through the crowd when they saw what was bearing down on them. A band of pixie musicians tossed aside their fiddles and harps and dived into a water trough to escape.

All around the market square, stalls stacked with jewels and amulets, and barrows piled high with strangely coloured fruit, were bashed into the air by the swaying sides of the speeding carriage. Goblins, ogres, leprechauns and other creatures made a desperate scramble for safety.

At last something caught the eye of the frenzied goats and they swerved towards it, panting greedily: a wagon overflowing with turnips.

Their hooves struck sparks off the road as they skidded to an abrupt halt just centimetres from their goal. Greg and Lewis were catapulted out of their seat. Tumbling head over heels through the air, they came down with a loud squish in a barrow of overripe bananas. The rear of the carriage bucked up in the air, then the whole vehicle slammed violently down on the ground. All four wheels split clean through and the entire left side broke apart, exposing Aunt Vivien and Lindsay, who were tangled in a dizzy heap.

Greg and Lewis hauled themselves out of the quagmire of squashed bananas, supporting each other until they were clear of the slippery expanse of yellow peel and sludge.

"That wasn't so bad!" Greg grinned.

"Yes, it was," Lewis groaned. "If the bananas hadn't broken our fall, we'd have multiple compound fractures and who knows what else."

Heedless of the mayhem they had caused, the goats shook loose of their halters and greedily gobbled down turnips. Lindsay took Aunt Vivien by the hand and helped her out of the wreckage.

Aunt Vivien's face was puffy and perspiring beneath her smeared make-up, and her elaborate hairdo, which the boys had always thought indestructible, was in ruins. That once proud edifice had collapsed into disarray and stray locks dangled before her eyes like vines trailing over a ruined temple.

"I'm covered in bruises from head to foot," she complained. "I've a good mind to make those animals into a stew."

"Where's the book?" Lewis asked when he saw that her hands were empty.

"Oh, I must have dropped it," Aunt Vivien realised.

Greg and Lewis pounced on the shattered carriage and made a frantic search. Lewis pulled the book out of the wreck and lofted it above his head in triumph.

"You keep it," Aunt Vivien told him. "I'm too exhausted. This day has proved to be something of an ordeal."

"You don't know the half of it!" Greg said.

A four foot tall brownie with pointed ears and a hooked nose appeared from behind the wagon. "My barrow! My turnips! Your goats!" he jabbered, hopping furiously from one foot to the other. "Very bad! Very bad!"

"Send the bill to Loki," Greg advised him, jabbing a thumb in the direction of the castle. "He'll pay you back tomorrow."

An ugly looking crowd was gathering around them, some of them armed with maces and chains.

"Ooh, Greg, there's a brawl brewing here," said Lindsay, taking to the air, "and you're not really equipped for it. You'd better follow me." Floating off, she led the way to the nearest exit from the square.

"Excuse us, folks," Greg apologised as he bustled his way past a burly centaur. "We have to get this woman to a hairdresser."

Lewis took Aunt Vivien by the elbow and steered

her speedily along in Greg's wake. Once they were clear of the market, they paused by a tree strung with tin kettles and spoons. Lewis opened the spellbook and flipped through the yellow pages.

"Aunt Vivien, can you find the spell we need?" he asked.

"You mean to start time moving again?" said Aunt Vivien. "Of course."

She plucked the book out of Lewis' hands and flipped back and forth several times before stopping at a particular page. "This is it here."

"Well, go ahead and do the hocus pocus," Greg urged. "We haven't got all day, you know."

Aunt Vivien laughed. "I can't do it here in the street, you sillies. I need the proper ingredients."

"Ingredients?" Lewis groaned.

Greg rolled his eyes despairingly.

"Yes, everybody knows that's how magic works," said Lindsay, alighting beside him.

"Powdered lizard bone, hummingbird wings," said Aunt Vivien, running a finger down the page, "a pinch of phoenix ash."

"And where are we going to get all that rubbish?" Greg demanded.

Aunt Vivien gave him a pitying look. "What are you getting so tetchy about? You'll find them in any well-stocked kitchen."

170

"In Mum's kitchen?" Lewis asked.

"Of course."

"Then what are we waiting for?" Greg fumed. "Let's go and make some magic."

They set out down Bridge Street then on up to Bannock Street. The house had just come into view when they heard a chillingly familiar sound from behind them. It was part bestial, part mechanical and wholly unmistakable. They turned and saw the Valkyries bearing down on them on their roadsteeds.

"Run!" Greg shouted.

They bolted for home, but Aunt Vivien – tottering along on her high heels – immediately began to fall behind. Greg and Lewis dropped back and took her by the arms to hurry her along. Lindsay flew above them, her wings fluttering desperately.

"We're not going to make it!" Lewis panted, casting a nervous glance over his shoulder. Shona Gilhooley was speeding ahead of her sisters, determined to wreak terrible vengeance upon the McBride boys.

"They are really getting up my nose!" Greg said through gritted teeth.

"The important thing is that Aunt Vivien gets to the kitchen," said Lewis.

"Right, so that makes us the rear guard."

The boys pulled up and Greg gave Aunt Vivien a

final shove. "Get to the house," he told her, "and cast the spell as fast as you can!"

Aunt Vivien hadn't the puff left to respond, but she lurched off, clutching the book to her bosom.

Greg and Lewis threw their arms up as the chief Valkyrie bore down on them like a thunderbolt.

"Leave them alone!" squealed Lindsay.

She swooped down into Shona's face, but as she did so, the warrior woman swung her sword and struck the fairy on the side of the head with the flat of the blade. Lindsay flopped to the ground, unconscious.

With a cry of dismay, Lewis started forward. Greg bounded after him, a split second too late to pull him back.

Shona's roadsteed reared up over them, front wheel buzzing like a chainsaw. Reining the creature in with her free hand, the Valkyrie brandished her sword in their faces. "Which of you will be the first to taste my steel?" she inquired with a cold smile.

Standing over Lindsay with his fists clenched, Lewis lost his temper. Without even thinking, he snatched the magic wand from Greg's belt and swung it as hard as he could.

It connected squarely with the tip of the roadsteed's nose. The wand's star-shaped headpiece exploded in a rainbow shower of sparks, as it unlocked all the mechanisms inside the metal mount. Its wheels buckled, its plates cracked apart, cogs, gears and screws went flying. With a ruinous clatter, the creature imploded into a heap of lifeless scrap, taking Shona down with it.

Veering off to avoid the wreckage, the other Valkyries crashed into one another and toppled over. Deaf to the curses Shona was shouting as she struggled to wriggle free, Lewis scooped up Lindsay and beat a speedy retreat.

"Nice work," Greg complimented him. "Let's go."

They sped off after Aunt Vivien, and caught up with her only a few metres from their driveway. "Not far now," Greg encouraged her on.

Suddenly there erupted a hideous din, like a pack of hellhounds baying for blood. The next instant, a hairy monster of nightmare proportions bounded over the neighbouring fence and planted itself squarely in their path.

"Oh no, the Larkins' dog!" Lewis exclaimed in horror.

The previous day, the animal had been a harmless, if noisy, mutt with no particular pedigree. Now it looked like three wolves rolled into one, with three sets of snapping jaws and a huge, bristling, six-legged body. Yellow saliva dripped from its fangs and its three sets of eyes blazed with a feral hunger.

Behind them a blood-curdling chorus of war cries rang out. The Valkyries were closing in on foot.

"Quick! Give me that!" cried Greg, and snatched the remains of the magic wand from Lewis' right hand.

"It's broken," Lewis objected. "It's no good for anything now."

"You think so?" Greg retorted. Turning to confront the Larkins' dog, he waved the wand over his head. "Here, boy!" he shouted. "Fetch!" And flung it as hard as he could.

All six of the monster dog's eyes fixed on the twirling stick and it bounded off in pursuit. The stick clattered to the ground in the midst of the startled Valkyries. The warrior women barely had time to shriek before the beast was upon them, scattering them like bowling pins.

Greg propelled Aunt Vivien towards the house while Lewis followed with Lindsay in his arms. Luckily, in her fairy form she was conveniently lightweight.

"That was pretty close to genius," Lewis said.

Greg gave him a smug look. "Did you expect anything less?"

"Frankly, yes," Lewis admitted.

"Thanks. Next time I'll toss you in the air and let the hound chase you."

They barged through the front door and on into the front room. Aunt Vivien promptly collapsed into the nearest armchair and began fanning herself with one plump, freckled hand. While Greg went back to secure the front door, Lewis carried Lindsay to the sofa and was startled to find it already occupied by the Chiz.

Arthur Chisholm was stretched out full length, with his hairy feet dangling over one end. His head was tilted back and he was snoring like a bulldozer.

Footsteps descended the stairs and Mum entered the room. "Arthur took a nasty knock on the head when those rude women knocked him over," she explained. "I insisted he come in and lie down, and he's been here ever since."

Seeing Aunt Vivien, she brightened, "Oh, Vivien, how was your date with Mr Key?" she asked coyly.

"Just let me tell you..." Aunt Vivien began in an outraged tone.

"Later!" Greg interrupted brusquely. "Right now you've got a spell to cook up in the kitchen."

"Spell?" Mum echoed. "What spell?"

"Come and help me, Adele," Aunt Vivien said, heaving herself to her feet. "While we're working, I'll tell you all about That Beast."

"You'd better take that poor girl upstairs," Mum told Lewis as she and Aunt Vivien made their exit. "You can put her in Greg's room."

The Chiz roused with a snort. "Greg?" he echoed groggily. "Target practice?"

"Not now, Chiz," said Greg. "We've got work to do and I need your help."

Lewis climbed the stairs carefully, doing his best not to jostle Lindsay as he carried her into Greg's room. He laid her out on the bed then gently removed her glasses so he could examine her head for signs of injury. There was a bump, but other than that it didn't look too bad.

Greg swept into the room and darted to the window. "The Larkins' dog is gone," he reported, "but the Valkyries are back. They're having some kind of argument – probably over who's going to lead the attack."

"Can we hold them off?" asked Lewis.

Greg shrugged. "Mum's locked all the windows and Chiz is barricading the doors. But it won't be long before they stop arguing and come after us."

Pushing past Lewis, he hunkered down and rummaged under his bed. When he stood up again, he had a golf club in hand.

"What good's that going to be against a broadsword?" Lewis said.

"You might be surprised," said Greg. "I think we can come up with a few tricks to even the odds."

"Do you think she's going to be all right?" Lewis asked, gazing anxiously down at Lindsay.

Greg bit back on the harsh comment that sprang to his lips and stood sympathetically over the unconscious fairy. "She'll be fine. She's magical, after all."

"Yes, she is." Lewis sighed.

At that moment Lindsay stirred and her eyes flickered open.

"You see, I told you," Greg said, throwing open the cupboard.

"What happened?" Lindsay asked in a daze.

"You got conked on the nut," Greg told her as he rummaged. "Lewis saved your life."

Lindsay's eyes widened and fixed on Lewis as though she were seeing him for the first time. "Lewis, you saved me?"

"It wasn't anything much," Lewis mumbled. His face turned bright red.

"Don't listen to him," Greg said, pulling a cycling helmet out of the closet. "He was a big hero."

"Oh, Lewis," said Lindsay.

She tried to sit up, but Lewis made her lie back down. "You stay here and rest," he told her. "You've taken a bad knock."

"That's right, just leave everything to us," said Greg. He strapped on the helmet and gestured with the golf club. "Come on, Lewis, we've got to hold them off till Aunt Vivien gets that spell working."

As the boys headed out the door, Lindsay's voice trilled, "Be careful, Lewis!"

Lewis looked back to where she was beaming at him. "I w-will," he stammered, then followed Greg down the stairs.

"Thanks," he said quietly when he caught up with his brother.

"Don't say I never did you a favour," said Greg.

Just then the house was shaken by a tremendous crash, as though someone had driven a battering ram into the front door.

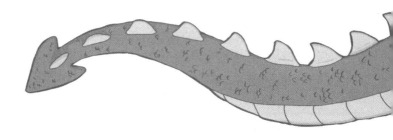

15. JUST ENOUGH COOKS

The brothers rushed to the hall where tables and chairs were piled up against the front door. The makeshift barricade was teetering under the impact of the blow. They heard a snort like steam escaping from a piston and the sound of a motorcycle engine revving furiously.

"They must be using one of those horse-bike things to smash the door!" cried Lewis.

"I hope it smashes its brains in!" Greg said between his teeth.

The Chiz appeared from behind them. "Back door blocked, Greg," he reported.

"That's great, Chiz," Greg said. "Help us out here, will you?"

The Chiz pressed his huge hands flat against the tottering mound of furniture and wedged it firmly back into place against the door.

The sharp crash of breaking glass sent them scurrying into the front room. Two Valkyries were climbing in through the window with swords at the ready. The Chiz surprised everyone by snatching up the sofa and heaving it at them with uncanny accuracy. With twin shrieks of dismay the Valkyries were bounced back into the front yard, leaving the sofa securely wedged in the window frame.

Greg crowed, "Top man, Chiz! I didn't think you had it in you!"

The Chiz's big face split in a gap-toothed grin. Thumping his hairy chest, he said proudly, "Did good."

Just then, there came a muffled boom from the rear of the house.

Greg clenched his golf club tightly. "Hold the fort here, Chiz," he said with a determined gleam in his eye. "I'll find out what they're up to. Lewis, go and see what's happening in the kitchen."

In the kitchen Aunt Vivien had her spellbook lying open on the counter in front of her. She was dropping ingredients into a pot of ooze that bubbled unpleasantly on the stove.

"How's the spell?" Lewis asked.

"We're getting there," Aunt Vivien replied, "but this has to be done ever so carefully."

Mum was standing with a pensive finger on her large, thick lip. "Goblin's fingernails, goblin's fingernails," she repeated to herself. "I'm sure we have some. Oh yes, I remember."

She reached up to a high shelf and brought down a pot.

"Could you speed it up?" Lewis pleaded. "We've not got much time."

Aunt Vivien ignored him and ran a finger along the next line in the book. "Let's see," she mused. "Iguana blood. Where do you keep that, Adele?"

The window over the sink suddenly shattered and a Valkyrie appeared. She sneered menacingly. In an instant Mum plucked a frying pan from the wall and walloped her square in the face, sending her flying backwards through the air.

"I'll thank you to stay out of my kitchen."

"Nice one, Mum!" Lewis gasped.

Aunt Vivien gave Lewis a warning glare. "Are you going to keep us gabbing all day, young man, or do you want this time business sorted out?"

A shout from Greg sent Lewis racing to join him. He found his brother pressed across a heap of trunks and boxes that reinforced the back door against the Valkyries' assault. Lewis added his weight to the pile as it shook under a renewed pounding.

After a few moments the attack stopped and the boys relaxed.

"How long do you think we can keep this up?" panted Lewis.

Greg straightened his cycling helmet and struck a commanding pose. "It's like Robert the Bruce said, *Swing like a spider and sting like a bee...*"

Lewis shook his head. "Nobody *ever* said that."

But Greg was already bolting towards the front door. Lewis joined him in time to see the barricade toppling like an avalanche. The door split down the middle and the metal head of a roadsteed thrust itself through the gap. With an angry roar of engines it began forcing its way into the house.

To Lewis' amazement Greg let out a wordless battle cry and charged forward, swinging his golf club. He brought a mighty blow down on the roadsteed's skull. The creature's glassy eyes popped out on a pair of springs, its body shuddered, and then it was still.

"Wow!" Lewis exclaimed. "You knocked it out!"

"Result!" Greg declared.

"Base wretch!" cried a familiar voice. "You will pay for slaying my steed."

Shona Gilhooley was clambering over the broken beast with the point of her sword thrust towards them.

"Get back, Greg!" Lewis warned. "She's on the warpath."

"No way, Lewis!" Greg responded. "I'm in the zone now."

With a wild cry of, "Fore!" he swung the golf club

and dashed the Valkyrie's sword from her grasp. Disarmed and dismayed, Shona gaped incredulously as her blade clattered across the floor. Greg flailed at her with the club and sent her scrambling backwards over her mount to safety.

"How's that for a workout!" Greg called after her as she fled.

Before he could savour his triumph, a riotous uproar broke out in the front yard. The brothers dashed up the stairs to their parents' bedroom to see what was going on.

Ignoring the tusks and antlers that now festooned the walls, they sped to the window and looked down. Below, the Valkyries and their remaining steeds were fleeing in terror from the Larkins' dog. It was tearing madly around the yard, snapping its three sets of slavering jaws at anything that moved.

"It must want to play some more," Greg said.

The din had finally roused Aunt Vivien's green dinosaur from its slumbers. It heaved itself sluggishly onto its stumpy legs and stood blinking sleepily at the surrounding chaos. After a moment, it gave a cavernous yawn and plodded off in search of a quieter neighbourhood, crushing fences and shrubbery in its path.

This did not distract the Larkins' three-headed

hound from its furious pursuit of the Valkyries, who were fleeing for safety in all directions.

Opening the window, Greg yelled, "Go get them, Fido!"

Lewis shook Greg's sleeve and pointed. "Look out! Here's more trouble!"

Two enormous trolls, each of them nearly ten feet tall, were jogging up the street, carrying a garishly-decorated sedan chair between them. They set it down on the pavement in front of the McBride house, where a familiar, green-clad figure climbed out.

"It's Loki!" exclaimed Lewis. "Now what are we going to do?"

Greg chewed his lip for a second. "Relax," he said. "I've got an idea."

He sprang to the door and shouted down the stairs, "Heads up, Chiz! I've got a job for you!"

He shouted a brief set of instructions before rejoining Lewis at the window. Shoulder to shoulder, they watched Loki straighten his jacket and adjust his fedora before entering the front garden.

The Larkins' dog was chasing off the last of the Valkyries when the creak of the gate caught its attention. First one head, then the other two whipped round in Loki's direction as he sauntered up the path. With a low growl the monster turned on the green-garbed intruder, three sets of dagger-teeth glittering dangerously.

Undaunted, Loki gave a casual snap of his fingers and a coil of flame appeared in his hand. With a flick of his wrist he sent the length of fire snaking through the air like a whip. The fiery lash connected with a crack, and the hound recoiled with a threefold yelp of pain.

The stink of scorched fur filled the air. Falling into a crouch, the monster dog glowered angrily at Loki with all six of its savage eyes. Loki lashed out again with his fiery whip and scored another hit.

With an anguished howl, the dog spun about and bolted with its tails between its legs. It disappeared around the back of the Larkin house, its pitiful yelps receding into the distance.

Loki opened his hand and the fire slithered back into his palm. "That takes care of the mutt," he said coolly.

Leaning out of the window, Greg called down, "You're hot stuff when it comes to dogs, *Lucas*, but an old lady can sneak up and whack you over the skull."

Loki whipped a cigar from his breast pocket and lit it with a flame that popped out of his thumb. "Don't waste your breath trying to insult me, kid," he snapped. "You're running out of time to make a deal and save your skin."

"Make a deal with you?" Greg scoffed. "I'd sooner kiss a tarantula."

Lewis watched nervously as Loki drew nearer, his jaw set in an angry grimace. "What are you winding him up for?" he pleaded in Greg's ear. "Aren't we in enough trouble?"

"I need him to come closer," Greg explained out of the side of his mouth.

The thud of heavy footsteps heralded the arrival of the Chiz. He had Mum's enormous washtub wrapped in his brawny arms and water sloshed about in it as he squeezed through the doorway. The brothers shifted aside to make room and the Chiz propped the tub against the window frame.

"Let me make this really simple for you, boys," snarled Loki. "Either you hand over the book or I burn your house to the ground with all of you in it."

"I don't think so," said Greg. "You see, we've got the book *and* Aunt Vivien, and that's more than enough to see off you and your conjuring tricks."

"Conjuring tricks!" Loki was seething now. He took a menacing step closer. "I'll show you tricks, you delinquent."

Taking a deep puff on his cigar, he exhaled a stream of sulfurous smoke that whirled about him like a storm cloud. A spark of lightning flashed from his finger and the cloud lit up like a bonfire. Unaffected by the flames, he advanced on the doorstep, blazing like a human torch.

"What's next?" Greg taunted. "Are you going to pull a rabbit out of your hat?"

"Next I'm going to turn you into a cinder!" Loki roared. "Laugh that off!"

Greg snorted contemptuously. "Face it, *Lucas*, we've been running rings around you all day. Why don't you pack it in and shuffle off back to Right Guard."

Loki glared up at him. "That's Asgard, you bonehead! *Asgard!*"

"Now, Chiz!" yelled Greg.

With a single heave, the Chiz upended the washtub over the windowsill. Several litres of water poured down in a deluge that broke over Loki like a waterfall. The flames guttered out with a loud hiss, leaving him drenched from head to foot.

Loki staggered back, swearing vehemently.

Greg let out a derisive hoot. "Nice going, Chiz!"

Loki gave himself a furious shake like a wet cat, and flung aside his extinguished cigar. "You'll pay for this, you worms!" he snarled as the steam rose from his suit. He snatched off his dripping hat and used it to wave the two trolls forward.

Greg turned to Lewis and the Chiz. "Let's go!" he ordered. "We have to keep them out of the kitchen!"

Scrambling downstairs, they reached the front hall in time to see the defunct roadsteed yanked out of the doorway and flung aside. One of the trolls bashed through the remains of the door and trampled the wrecked barricade under its oversized feet.

"Leave this to me!" said Greg, taking a tight grip on his golf club.

"No!" Lewis cried. He could see that Greg was in such a rush he wasn't thinking straight.

He charged the troll and whacked it hard. The impact jarred him from head to toe as the golf club snapped in two and fell from his numbed fingers. The troll hadn't even felt the blow. It raised a massive fist to crush Greg, who was now backing frantically away.

"Help him, Chiz!" yelled Lewis.

Lumbering forward, the Chiz threw his arms around the troll and they lurched from side to side, bashing off the walls in a monster wrestling match. While they grappled, noises of rending and tearing came from the front room.

"Whatever you do, Chiz, don't let go!" called Greg as he and Lewis rushed to investigate.

The second troll had punched the sofa out of the window and sent it bouncing across the floor. Then the monster crashed into the room like a runaway train, scattering bricks in all directions, the broken window frame dangling around its neck.

The brothers reeled back as the troll barrelled across the floor and crashed head first into the opposite wall. The force of the collision shook the whole house. The troll lumbered backwards to collapse in a senseless heap among the bricks and dust.

"He's knocked himself out!" Lewis exclaimed in relief.

"See, I told you everything would be okay," said Greg.

The next instant, the Chiz came tumbling in from the hallway, bowling the brothers aside. He flopped down on top of the unconscious troll and lay there stunned. The other troll tromped in after him, its tiny eyes blazing with berserk fury, its fist still swinging.

With no other weapon handy, Greg snatched off his cycling helmet and hurled it with all his might. It bounced harmlessly off the troll's chest. Lewis shook the Chiz's arm in desperation. "Chiz, wake up! We need you!" he yelled.

The Chiz began to snore.

Roaring with rage, the pursuing troll advanced on the brothers, brandishing its rock-like knuckles. Greg yanked Lewis out of range and barked, "Fall back to the kitchen!"

Clambering over the Chiz and the unconscious

troll, they tumbled into the kitchen, slamming the door behind them. They were engulfed by a cloud of malodorous steam, through which they could see Mum and Aunt Vivien hovering over the stove.

"Aunt Vivien! The spell!" Lewis panted. "You've got to say it *now!*"

On the stove top an iron pot bubbled and burped. The toxic reek it gave off made them glad of the breeze wafting in through the broken window.

With a curt nod Aunt Vivien waved her hands over the pot and peered hard at the book that lay on the counter beside her. Brow furrowed in concentration, she began chanting the spell. To Lewis the unintelligible words sounded like a duet between a whale and a cuckoo.

From the far room came the ominous thud of approaching feet.

"Chant faster!" urged Greg. "Here, Lewis, give me a hand!"

The fridge had been transformed into a large metal chest, which the boys now shoved into place against the door. There was a light knock and Loki called, "Anybody in there?"

"We've gone to the beach!" Greg answered. "We'll be back on Tuesday."

There was a heartbeat's pause. Then, without

warning, the door was smashed clean off its hinges by a resounding blow that knocked the metal chest right across the room. Greg and Lewis were sent sprawling. Elbowing himself up dazedly, Lewis saw the troll looming on the threshold, fist upraised to strike again. Waving the creature aside, Loki stepped around it into the kitchen. "My, my," he drawled. "What's cooking?"

"A load of trouble for you," Greg puffed belligerently from the floor.

"Give that big mouth a rest, kid," Loki retorted. "I'm talking to the ladies."

Frostily ignoring him, Aunt Vivien carried on chanting. Mum turned around, planting her ogrish bulk directly in front of him. Pointing at the ruined door, she said crossly, "I hope you plan on replacing that."

"First things first," said Loki with a confident smirk. Turning to Aunt Vivien, he snapped, "Cut that out, Viv, before you do yourself an injury."

Aunt Vivien raised her voice, straining to pronounce the harsh syllables. The brothers sensed that her chant was building to a crescendo.

Greg staggered to his feet, pulling Lewis up with him. "Face it, Loki, you're done!" he challenged.

Loki eyed him with cool contempt. "Not till the fat lady's finished her song," he retorted, "and that's not happening." Turning to the troll, he pointed a finger at Aunt Vivien. "Silence that overweight canary," he ordered, and stepped aside.

The troll bulled its way into the kitchen. Shouldering Mum out of its path, it swept Aunt Vivien off her feet. Her squawk of indignation was stifled by a scaly palm the size of a dinner plate clamping itself over her mouth.

Greg and Lewis seized the troll's arms in an effort to free her, only to find themselves hauled off the floor, their legs dangling. Lewis' gaze fell upon the hourglass standing on the counter where the egg-timer used to be. Most of the sand was in the top half and there was no sign of movement. Time was still frozen. Aunt Vivien's eyes bulged urgently, sending out a mute appeal to the boys. Swinging like a pendulum, Greg aimed a kick between the troll's squat legs. He might as well have been kicking a brick wall.

Loki swaggered over to the stove and eyed the magical brew, which was bubbling furiously in its pot. "I think I'd better pour this away before it goes off," he drawled. He spotted the spellbook lying on the counter and seized it with a grin. "I'll take care of this too."

There was a flicker of light and Lindsay appeared, hovering in the air above them. She looked a little dizzy.

"I tried to take a nap like you told me, Lewis," she said, "but honestly, the *noise*!"

Still gripping the troll's arm, Lewis's glance lighted on the spice rack just behind where Loki was standing. Amongst the transformed contents was a glass jar of rusty powder that looked like cayenne pepper.

Pointing, he said, "Lindsay, do you see that jar of red powder there?"

Lindsay nodded then clutched her head as though it hurt.

"Toss it to me!"

Lindsay ducked behind Loki and snatched the jar from the rack. As she fluttered away, Loki took a swipe at her with the book and missed. "I should have brought a fly swatter," he snapped irritably.

"Here, Lewis," said Lindsay, lobbing the jar towards him.

Lewis caught it in one hand and waved it in front of the troll. "Hey, big boy, you look hungry!" he shouted. "Here's a treat for you!"

The troll's piggy eyes widened greedily. It opened its maw and Lewis tossed the jar inside. Before Loki could intervene, its massive teeth crunched down, pulverizing the container and releasing its contents.

The troll went rigid. Eyes popping wide, it made a noise like an elephant choking on a peppermint. Then it let out a massive sneeze.

The blast shook the air, throwing Loki off balance

and knocking the book out of his hands. Lindsay was whirled into a spin that landed her, winded and dazed, in the sink. Greg and Lewis were flung aside as the troll continued sneezing. Aunt Vivien dropped to the floor as a climactic nasal detonation knocked the creature clear off its feet.

She landed flat on her belly, right beside the spellbook. Propping herself up on her elbows, she fixed her gaze on the last lines of the spell and rapped them out in a gabble of magical syllables.

Loki made a desperate lunge to knock the pot off the stove, but before he could reach it, the contents exploded in a dazzling blast that rocked the house and sent them all reeling.

Lewis heard Loki curse through the clouds of blue smoke that billowed across the kitchen. As the air cleared, he saw Greg latch onto the table to steady himself. Mum and Aunt Vivien were clinging together, their faces buried in each other's shoulders. Lindsay coughed and curled up in the sink with her arms over her head.

Lewis' eyes darted to his watch. With a whoop of delight he saw the numbers changing rapidly. "It worked!" he cried.

His jubilation turned to horror when he saw Loki make a leap for the book, which was still lying open on the floor. Lewis made a desperate grab, but Loki was faster and caught it up in both hands.

"Game's not over yet, boys," he declared. "I can just cast the spell all over again." He blew a mock kiss at Aunt Vivien. "Thanks for showing me the ropes, Viv."

"You unspeakable cad," Aunt Vivien responded with a venomous glower.

"Correct me if I'm wrong," said Greg, "but won't you need to collect the ingredients for your spell first?"

Loki shrugged. "That's a piece of cake, kid."

"But a cake needs time to bake," said Greg with a smirk.

He pointed at the hourglass. The sand was running down swiftly and in seconds it had all dropped to the bottom. Lewis flipped it over. Again an hour's worth of sand ran out in a matter of seconds.

"What in blazes is going on?" Loki demanded.

The numbers on Lewis' watch were racing so fast now they had become a blur. "Time hasn't just started up again," he explained excitedly, "it's hurrying to catch up with itself!"

"And it's catching up with you too, Loki," Greg added with relish. "Lokiday's over at last."

Loki turned white. Wheeling, he thrust the spellbook at Aunt Vivien. "Make this stop, Viv! Please!" he begged. "I'll make it worth your while, I promise."

Aunt Vivien tottered proudly on her high heels. She snatched the book away from him and said, "You and I have nothing more to say to each other, Lucas. You're nothing but a –" she struggled to find a suitably damning word, "– a chancer!"

Loki looked stunned. His eyes swivelled to the window and his mouth dropped open in disbelief.

The sun shot overhead like a rocket, drawing light and shadow behind it in a darkening curtain. The moon followed like a silver plate hurled across the heavens, flashing from east to west as stars popped out all over the sky.

In the deepening twilight Greg's triumphant grin was still clearly visible. "Cheerio, Loki!" he said. "It's time to kiss your day goodbye."

A final Nordic curse sprang to Loki's lips, then everything went black.

16. GOOD LUCK AND GOOD RIDDANCE

There was a knock at the bedroom door and Mum's voice called, "Wake up, boys! It's a school day!"

Lewis heard her walk away towards the stairs as he stirred from his sleep. He extracted an arm from the sleeping bag and reached for his watch. The display read 7:34.

Greg was invisible beneath his mound of disordered covers. Lewis stretched over and gave him a poke. He was answered by a grunt, then Greg sat bolt upright, the covers falling into a heap on the floor. He looked down at Lewis.

"What day is it?"

"Friday I hope," Lewis answered.

Greg jumped out of bed and yanked open the curtains. He looked at the back garden in the fresh morning light and nodded his head. There was no sign of the well or anything else out of the ordinary. "It looks normal," he murmured.

He rounded on Lewis with a suspicious gleam in

his eye. "You don't think I'm cracked in the head, do you?"

"No, I remember it all too," Lewis reassured him. "Lokiday, Loki, everything."

"So it really did happen."

Greg crossed the room and poked his head out into the hallway.

"Everything seems to be back to normal," he said.

They got dressed and hurried downstairs for breakfast. They stopped at the kitchen door, briefly paralysed by the memory of yesterday's experiences. They could hear Mum singing "All You Need Is Love".

It was Lewis who worked up the nerve to open the door and walk into the kitchen. Mum was there in a white blouse and a pair of jeans, her light brown hair tied with a ribbon at the back. She looked round and smiled.

"Mum, you're not an ogre!" Lewis exclaimed.

Mum looked at him as though he were ill. "Should I take that as a compliment?"

"What's for breakfast?" Greg asked.

"Bacon and eggs. Is that all right?"

"It's better than all right, Mum."

"Fine. Help yourself to some cereal."

They poured themselves a generous helping of sugared nut flakes by way of celebration and sat down to eat. Even the milk tasted better than ever.

"You know, after all that madness, having Aunt Vivien visit doesn't seem like such a big problem any more," Lewis said.

Greg almost choked on his flakes. "What?" he exclaimed, staring at his brother.

Lewis shook his head. "You're right. I don't know what made me say that."

"You boys seem very excited this morning," Mum said when she came out with the bacon and eggs.

"Of course we are," Lewis told her. "It's Friday."

As they headed off to school they were pleased to note a complete absence of horses, goats, giant frogs, goblins, trolls, fairies and, above all, Valkyries. They had to cut short their discussion of the previous day's events when they ran into Tim Findlay and the Nicoll kids, and they didn't see each other again until school finished.

Greg strolled out of the gate and spotted Lewis talking to Lindsay. He had never seen this before, and it was so curious it drew him in spite of his powerful instinct to avoid Lindsay at all costs.

"Are you two talking about me?" he asked jauntily.

Lindsay barely looked at him. She said, "Hi, Greg," in an off-hand manner and turned back to Lewis. "I'll see you later, Lewis," she beamed, then skipped off down the street.

"Yes, good," Lewis said, looking more bewildered than happy.

"What happened?" Greg asked him. "Did you finally use those hypnosis techniques I told you about?"

Lewis shook his head. "She's been following me around all day, just making conversation. She even told me she was going to the skating rink tomorrow and that I should come along."

"Rather you than me," Greg said wryly.

Lewis blushed. "I don't know what's going on. She can't remember anything that happened on Lokiday. Nobody except us does. Probably not even Loki."

"Maybe it's just your natural charm shining through at last. If you'd watched that DVD *Seventeen Steps to Self-confidence* like I told you to last year, this would have happened a long time ago. But no, you were too wet."

"So how did the maths test go?" Lewis asked, changing the subject.

Greg's grin was so wide Lewis wondered what was keeping his jaw in place. "It was cancelled. Mrs Witherspoon came down with flu and had to stay at home. Can you believe it?"

The Chiz came loping past and waved a greeting.

"Chiz, how about some target practice later?" Greg suggested.

"Huh?" The Chiz stared at him, baffled.

"Never mind. I'm just kidding."

The Chiz ambled off. He looked better without the fur.

Greg and Lewis strolled home at a leisurely pace, still enjoying the fact that it was Friday. When they reached the house, what they didn't see brought them to a dramatic halt.

"Where's Aunt Vivien's car?" Lewis asked.

Greg shrugged. "It's not like anybody would steal such an atrocity."

Once inside, they cornered Mum in the front room.

"Where's Aunt Vivien?" they asked in unison.

"She got a call from a sick friend and had to leave," Mum answered. "Her neighbour, Letitia, I think it was."

Her own relief was poorly disguised.

Greg gave his brother a wink. "See? I told you it would be a lucky day."

They went upstairs to Greg's room and Lewis began gathering his stuff together. He stopped when he came to Loki's book, *The Folklore Of Time*. He picked it up tentatively, as if it were packed with high explosives.

"What do you think we should do about this?" he asked. "Suppose somebody else recites the rhyme."

Greg took the book from him and flipped to the Lokiday rhyme. Taking a firm grip on the top of the page, he ripped it right out.

Lewis couldn't contain his shock at seeing a book mutilated like this. "You can't do that!" he exclaimed. "What will I tell Mr Calvert when he sees there's a page missing?"

Greg smiled. "Tell him I ate it."

And he did.

Meanwhile, in Las Vegas, a red-haired figure in an expensive green suit was being ejected from the Three Horseshoes Casino by two burly individuals who were not in the habit of being argued with. The red-haired man picked himself up from the pavement and dusted off his suit.

"My credit's still good in plenty of joints in this town!" he shouted at the two hulking figures as they disappeared inside the casino. "I don't have to cheat there!"

He stood and fumed for a moment then stuffed his hands into his pockets before stalking off down the brightly lit boulevard. Passers-by gave way to him, as though there were a red warning light blinking on the top of his head.

A light sprinkle of rain began to fall, prompting him to turn up his collar and tug down the brim of his fedora. "Cleaned out again," he muttered sourly to himself. "You'd think that just once I could get one tiny piece of good luck."

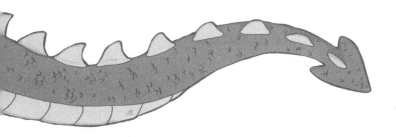

Mischievous fairies? Smelly troll?
Werewolf snatching your sheep?
Email the Really Weird Removals company!

Luca and Valentina's Uncle Alistair runs the Really
Weird Removals company, a pest control business to
catch supernatural creatures! When the children join
Alistair's team they befriend a lonely ghost, rescue a
stranded sea serpent, and trap a cat-eating troll.

But the paranormal world is also packed with danger and
secrets. Will Luca and Valentina discover more than they
can handle?

 Also available as an eBook

reallyweirdremovals.com

43 missing cats (and counting!)
2 feline observation operatives
1 time-twisting manhole cover

Fergus can't believe it when his brand-new digital watch starts going backwards. Then he crashes (literally) into gadget-loving Murdo and a second mystery comes to light: cats are going missing all over the neighbourhood.

 Also available as an eBook

discoverkelpies.co.uk

Why did the chicken cross the road?
TO TAKE OVER THE WORLD!!!

Giant robot chickens are terrorising the city of Aberdeen. Their aim: to peck out all signs of human resistance.

Jesse and his friends hatch a plan to stop the fowl fiends and take back their city...

Life in a chicken apocalypse isn't all it's cracked up to be!

 Also available as an eBook

discoverkelpies.co.uk

THE
MAGNUS
FIN
TRILOGY

Three exciting underwater adventures
starring Magnus Fin, the eleven-year-old
half-selkie (part-human, part-seal) hero.

 Also available as eBooks

discoverkelpies.co.uk